# THE BARKING GHOST

Look for other **Goosebumps**® books
by R.L. Stine:

# Goosebumps®

# THE BARKING GHOST

## R.L. STINE

SCHOLASTIC INC.
New York Toronto London Auckland Sydney
Mexico City New Delhi Hong Kong Buenos Aires

ISBN 0-439-56825-0

Copyright © 1995 by Scholastic Inc.

12 11 10 9 8 7 6 5 4 3 2 1          3 4 5 6 7 8/0

Printed in the U.S.A.                                40

First Scholastic printing, June 1995

# THE BARKING GHOST

For the zillionth time that night, I threw the covers off my legs and bolted up from the bed.

I definitely heard something that time.

And it wasn't the wind, either. I'm always hearing things. But no matter what I hear, Mom says, "It's just the wind, Cooper. Just the wind."

But the wind doesn't sound like heavy footsteps crunching through the leaves. And that's what I heard this time. Definitely.

I stood next to my bedroom window. Then I leaned over and peered out. It sure was spooky out there.

I squinted to see better in the dark. Don't lean over too far, I thought. Don't let whoever or *whatever* is out there see you.

My eyes searched the backyard. I lifted my head — and spotted them. A few feet away. Huge, black, gnarly arms. Reaching out toward the window.

Ready to grab me.

No. It was only the branches of the old oak tree.

Well, give me a break. I *said* it was dark out!

My eyes swept over the yard again. The sound. There it was!

I ducked. My legs trembled as I crouched beneath the window. I broke out into a cold sweat.

*Crunch. Crunch.*

Even louder than before.

I swallowed hard and took another peek. Something moved in the shadows. Under the oak tree. I held my breath.

*Crunch. Crunch, crunch.*

A gust of wind blew the tree branches furiously.

*Crunch, crunch, crunch.*

The frightening sounds grew louder. Closer to the house.

As I peered out, two eyes suddenly flashed in the dark. My throat went dry. I couldn't cry out.

The eyes flashed again. They were even closer to the house this time. Right outside my window.

Staring at me.

Moving toward me.

The creature's dark shape began to take form. It was a —

— bunny rabbit??

I let out a long sigh.

The first night in my new house — and I was already shaking in terror.

I shuffled into the bathroom for a towel. As I mopped the sweat from my forehead, I stared at my reflection in the medicine chest mirror.

Whenever I'm scared, my freckles really stand out. There they were. Millions of them.

I ran my fingers through my hair. I wear it long. To help cover my big, droopy ears.

I've had these huge ears my whole life. Mom keeps telling me not to worry. She says I'll grow into them. But I'm twelve now, and nothing has changed. My ears are still huge. Huge and droopy.

I wear a cap most of the time to help hide them. It's my favorite cap from my favorite baseball team — the Red Sox. So I don't mind wearing it.

A bunny rabbit, I mumbled as I stared at myself in the mirror. Scared by a bunny rabbit.

I'd made it through the entire day without being scared once. That's pretty good for me.

Back where I used to live — in Boston, Massachusetts — my best friends, Gary and Todd, always made fun of me.

"Cooper," they'd say, "you probably scare *yourself* on Halloween!"

They were right. I get scared a lot. Some people just scare easier than others. I'm an easy scarer.

Take last summer at camp. I got lost in the woods on my way to the bathroom cabin. What did I do?

Nothing. I just stood there.

3

When the kids from my bunk finally found me, I was shaking all over. Practically in tears. Turns out I was standing a few feet from the dining hall the whole time.

So, okay. I admit it. When it comes to bravery, I'm not exactly Indiana Jones!

When my parents announced we were moving from the city into a house in the woods, I was a little tense.

Maybe even scared.

Scared to leave the apartment I'd lived in my entire life.

Scared of a house in the woods.

And then I learned that our new house was *deep* in the woods, somewhere in Maine. Miles from the nearest town.

The only two scary books I'd ever read took place in Maine. In the woods.

But I had no choice. We were moving. Mom's new job landed us in Maine, and there was nothing I could do about it.

I left the bathroom and crept back to my bed. The floorboards creaked and cracked with each step. It was going to be hard getting used to that.

It was also going to be hard getting used to all the other strange noises this old house made. The rattling pipes. The scraping shutters. And some weird noise that thumped really loudly every hour.

At dinner, Mom said that the thumping noise was only the house "settling."

Whatever that means.

At least she didn't say, "It's just the wind, Cooper."

I jumped into bed and pulled the covers up to my chin. Then I fluffed my pillows two or three times, trying hard to get comfortable. I felt a little safer in bed.

I love my bed. Mom wanted to trash it when we moved. She said I needed a new one. But I said no way. It had taken me years to break this bed in. The mattress had just the right amount of lumps, and they were in all the right spots.

In the dark, I glanced around my new room. It was so weird seeing all my things in this strange place. When the movers carried my stuff in here this morning, I had them put the furniture exactly the way it was in my old room.

Across from my bed, my dad built a really cool bookcase for all my snow domes. It has a light in it and everything.

I can't wait to unpack my snow domes. I have seventy-seven of them from all over the world — even Australia and Hong Kong. I guess you could call me a snow dome collector.

Anyway, I was finally beginning to relax, thinking about my snow domes — when I heard another noise.

Not a bunch of little crunches like before — but one long, drawn-out crunch.

I shot straight up in bed. This time I was sure. One hundred percent sure. Someone — or something — was creeping around out there. Right outside my window!

I threw off the covers. Then I dropped to the floor on my hands and knees. Moving slowly, I crawled to the window. Then I carefully pulled myself up and peered outside.

What was it?

A snake?

I flung open the window. I grabbed a softball from the floor and tossed it at the snake. Then I fell back down to my knees and listened.

Silence. No crunching. No slithering.

A direct hit. Great!

I stood and leaned carefully out the window. I was feeling pretty proud of myself. After all, I had just saved my family from a deadly —

— garden hose!

I let out a disappointed sigh and shook my head. Get a grip, Cooper.

If Gary and Todd were here, they would never let me hear the end of this. They'd be laughing their heads off.

"Nice going, Coop!" Gary would say. "Saved your family from a poisonous garden hose!"

"Yeah. Super Cooper strikes again!" Todd

would say. Back in bed again, I fluffed up my pillows one more time. Then I closed my eyes as tightly as I could.

That's it, I said to myself. I am *not* getting up again. I don't care what I hear next.

I will not get up from this bed again. No matter what.

And then I heard another noise. A different kind of noise. A sound that made my heart pound right through my chest.

Breathing.

Deep, heavy breathing.

In my room.

Under my bed!

# 2

I didn't move.

I *couldn't* move.

I stared at the ceiling. Listening. Listening to the raspy breathing under my bed.

Okay, Cooper, I told myself. Calm down. It's probably your imagination. Playing tricks on you again.

The breathing grew louder. Raspier.

I covered my ears and shut my eyes tight.

It's nothing. It's nothing. It's nothing.

It's an old house, I thought, still covering my ears. Old houses have to breathe — don't they?

Or, what was it that Mom said? Settling? Yeah, that's what it must be. The house settling.

Or maybe it's the pipes. We had pipes in our apartment in Boston, and they made crazy noises all the time. I'll bet that's what it is — the pipes.

I lowered my hands.

Silence now. No settling. No pipes. No breathing.

I must be losing my mind.

If I told Gary and Todd about this one, they'd really laugh their heads off.

And then the breathing started again. Raspy and wet. Hoarse breathing. Like a sick animal.

I couldn't just lie there. I had to see what it was.

I swung my legs out of bed. I took a deep breath. Then I lowered myself to the floor.

Carefully, I lifted the blanket from the bottom of the bed. Then carefully, carefully, I lowered my head and peeked under the bed.

That's when the hands darted out — and grabbed me. Two strong, cold hands. Slowly tightening their grip around my throat.

# 3

I screamed.

So loudly, I surprised myself.

My attacker must have been surprised, too. He quickly let go of my neck. I clutched my throat and sputtered for air.

"Cooper, will you keep it down?" a voice whispered. "You'll wake Mom and Dad!"

Huh?

Oh, man.

It was Mickey. My totally obnoxious older brother.

"Mickey! You jerk!" I cried. "You scared me to death!"

Mickey slid out from under the bed and wiped some dust off his pajamas. "No big challenge," he muttered.

"Shut up," I snapped, rubbing my sore neck. In the mirror I could see where Mickey's hands had grabbed my throat. Dark red blotches circled my neck.

"Look what you did!" I cried. "You *know* I bruise easily!"

"Oh, don't be such a baby! I got you, man!" Mickey cried, grinning.

I stared furiously at my idiot brother. I wished I could wipe that grin off his face. And not get in trouble for it.

"You're a jerk!" was all I could think to say.

"Grow up!" Mickey shot back. He headed for the door, then turned around. "Would Cooper like a little night-light next to his bed?" he asked in a tiny baby voice.

That's when I lost it.

I leaped on to his back and pounded his head with my fists.

"Hey!" he screamed, trying to shake me off. "What do you think you're doing? Get off me!"

Mickey's legs buckled under him, and he fell to the floor. I clung to his back. I kept pounding him with my fists.

Mickey is three years older than me, and he's a lot bigger. But I had him in the right position, and landed a few good punches.

Then he shifted to the right.

And started pounding me back. Luckily, he got

in only one really good wallop before Mom and Dad ran in to break it up.

"Cooper! Mickey! What's going on in here?"

"He started it!" I called out, trying to duck Mickey's fists.

My father reached down and pulled Mickey off me. "I don't care who started it!" he said angrily. "This is no way to act on the first night in your new house. Mickey, get back to your room!"

"But, Dad, he — "

"Never mind who started it. This behavior had better stop — now! Because if there is a *next* time, you'll both start off the new school year grounded!"

Grumbling, Mickey stomped out of the room. But not before sticking his tongue out at me. Mickey was the baby. Not me.

"Really, Dad, Mickey started it," I said when he was gone.

"And you're totally innocent, right?" my father asked, rolling his eyes.

"Yes!" I insisted.

Dad just shook his head. "Go to sleep, Cooper."

When my parents left the room, I paced back and forth, rubbing my neck.

I was so steamed!

It wasn't the first time Mickey's pulled something like this. For as long as I can remember,

Mickey has played tricks on me, trying to terrify me.

He usually succeeds, too.

Once, when Mom and Dad went away for a weekend, he hid a tape recorder in my room. It played horrifying screams all night long.

And another time, he didn't come to get me after Little League practice. He left me standing there, all alone on the playground, while he hid out and watched me panic.

But hiding under my bed tonight was the worst. He has to be one of the biggest jerks alive.

I climbed back into bed and stared up at the ceiling. I had to think of a way to get Mickey back.

What could I do? Hide outside his window and scream?

Jump out from behind the shower curtain when he's brushing his teeth?

No. Too dumb. It would have to be something totally excellent. Something so creepy it would scare me. Even though I was the one doing it.

I watched the spooky shadows move along my walls and ceiling. And listened to the frightening noises of my new house — noises I would have to hear for the rest of my life.

The pipes rattling. The dogs barking.

Wait a minute.

Dogs?

I sat up. We don't have a dog. And there isn't another house around here for miles.

But I definitely heard a barking dog.

I listened closely. The dog barked again. Then started to howl.

I sighed and pulled off the covers again. I started to climb out of bed. Then it hit me.

Mickey!

This had to be another one of my brother's stupid tricks. He was an excellent dog-barker. He practiced it all the time.

Smiling, I settled back on my pillow. I wouldn't get up. I wouldn't go to the window.

He wasn't going to get me this time. No way.

I lay there listening to Mickey make a fool of himself. Howling and barking like a big old dog.

What a jerk.

Then, suddenly, I sat up again. Whoa. I heard *two* dogs howling now.

Even Mickey couldn't pull that off.

The howling turned to piercing cries. So close. Right under my window.

As I said, I made it through a whole day without being scared. But, boy, was I making up for it tonight!

For the zillionth and third time, I slowly crept

to the window. I could hear them clearly. Two dogs. Wailing and howling.

For the zillionth and third time, I gazed out the window.

But for the *first* time, I couldn't believe what I saw.

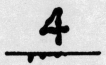

# 4

I didn't see anything.

Nothing at all. No dogs. Not one.

I squinted into the yard. Empty.

How could they have vanished so quickly?

I stood at the window for a few more seconds, but no dogs appeared.

I shivered. I'll never sleep again, I thought. Not as long as I have to live here.

I crept back to bed. I pulled the covers up to my chin. And counted the green and blue squigglies on the wallpaper by my head.

I guess I finally fell asleep. When I opened my eyes, light streamed in through my window.

Yawning, I glanced at the clock. Six-thirty. I'm usually an early bird. I like to start my day as soon as possible.

I leaped out of bed and checked the yard. It didn't seem half as scary in the morning light.

I smiled when I noticed the jungle gym in the

far corner. The last owners of the house built it. It had a slide and really high monkey bars. Yesterday, Dad hung a rope and tire from one of its beams, so now it had a swing, too.

Behind the jungle gym, the woods stretched all around. Woods thick with all different kinds of trees and shrubs and weeds. The woods surrounded our house on three sides. It seemed to go on forever.

I changed quickly, pulling a clean Red Sox T-shirt over my jeans. Grabbing my baseball cap, I flew through the house and ran outside.

A great summer day! Sunny and warm. If I were back home in Boston, I would hop on my bike and ride over to Gary's or Todd's house. Then we would spend the day outdoors, playing softball at the playground. Or just messing around.

But I'm not in Boston anymore. Better get used to that, I told myself.

I hoped some cool kids lived in this neighborhood. When we drove up to our house yesterday, I didn't see any other houses around. I guessed I'd have to spend the next few days alone — until school started next week.

I wandered over to the jungle gym. I swung on the tire swing for a little while. Back and forth. Back and forth. Staring at my bedroom window from the outside. Back and forth. Back and forth. Remembering last night.

Remembering just how brave Super Cooper had been. Yuck!

Back and forth. Back and forth.

Remembering the dogs.

Hey. That's weird, I thought. Those dogs I heard should have left paw prints all over the yard. But I couldn't see a single one.

I hopped off the swing and searched the ground all around the house. No sign of any dogs.

That's funny. I *knew* there were dogs out here last night.

I glanced up at the edge of the woods. Maybe those dogs were lost, I thought. Maybe they came to the house last night searching for help.

Maybe I should go track them down.

I bit my lower lip. A kid could lose his way — forever — in those woods, I thought nervously.

Well, I'm going in, I decided. Today is the first day of the new me. Super Cooper — for real. I wanted to find those dogs. To prove to myself that I wasn't going crazy.

Who knows? If I find the dogs, maybe Dad will let me keep one, I decided. It might be fun to have a dog.

I'd always wanted a puppy. But Mom said the fur made her sneeze. Maybe she'd change her mind.

I took one long, deep breath. Then I stepped into the woods. I saw some amazing trees. I saw

18

beautiful old birch trees with smooth, white trunks. And I saw sassafras and maple trees. Their trunks were gnarled and thick.

They could be over a hundred years old, I thought. Awesome.

Maybe Dad can build a tree house back here, I told myself excitedly. That would be so cool. Then when Gary and Todd came to visit, we could hang out in it.

I kept my eyes on the ground as I walked, searching for any sign of dogs.

Nothing. No prints. No broken branches.

How weird. I definitely heard dogs last night.

Or maybe I just *thought* I'd heard those dogs. It *was* kind of late, and I *was* pretty sleepy. Maybe it was my imagination.

Or maybe it was Mickey after all.

Maybe he tape-recorded another dog and barked along with it.

He would do something like that.

He's that sneaky.

I really had to pay him back. Something way creepy. Maybe I could do something out here in the woods.

I made my way through the thick trees and tall weeds, the whole time thinking of how to scare Mickey.

I suddenly realized I hadn't been paying attention to where I was going.

I spun around and peered through the thick trunks.

My house! I couldn't see it!

Okay, Cooper, keep cool. You can't be that far away, I told myself.

But my palms began to sweat.

I swallowed hard, then tried to remember which way I'd come.

Definitely the left.

No, wait. Maybe right.

I hung my head and moaned. It's no use, I thought.

I'm lost. Hopelessly lost.

# 5

I really didn't want to cry.

Who needed Mickey seeing me with wet, red eyes?

I'd never hear the end of it.

Besides, today was the first day of the new me. The new Super Cooper.

I took a really deep breath and tried to calm down.

I decided to walk a little to my right. If I didn't see my house, I'd turn and double back to the left.

It was worth a try.

What did I have to lose? I was lost anyway.

I turned to the right. I tried to take the straightest path possible.

The snapping of branches behind me made me spin around.

No one there.

It's just a harmless squirrel or something, I told myself. Just keep going.

I returned to my straight path again. But with my first step, I heard leaves rustling behind me.

I didn't turn around. I quickened my pace.

And I heard it again.

Twigs snapping. Leaves rustling.

My throat suddenly felt dry. Don't panic. Don't panic. "Wh-who's there?" I croaked.

No answer.

I turned back.

Whoa! Which way had I been walking? My head began to spin. I suddenly felt dizzy. Too dizzy to remember where I had been.

*Snap. Snap. Crack. Crunch.*

"Who is there?" I called out again. My voice didn't sound all that steady for Super Cooper.

"Mickey, is that you? This isn't funny! Mickey?"

Then I felt something horrible scrape my cheek. Something cold. And sharp.

I couldn't help it. I started to scream.

# 6

A leaf. A dumb leaf.

Come on, Cooper! Get a grip!

I sat down on the ground for a second. I checked my watch. It was almost eight.

Dad would be out in the yard soon. He planned to set up the new barbecue grill first thing this morning. I figured I could just wait for the hammering to start, then walk in the direction of the noise.

I'd just sit here. And wait. Wait for the hammering. Good idea, I thought.

I heard something rustle behind me.

Just the leaves, I told myself. The dumb leaves.

I stole a glance up at the trees. I tilted my head way back — and someone grabbed my arm.

I jerked away. Sprang up. Started to run.

And tripped over my own feet.

Scrambling up, I gasped in surprise.

A girl.

She was about my age and had really long, red hair. It was frizzy, and it stuck out in a million directions. She had big green eyes. She wore a bright red T-shirt and red shorts. She reminded me of a rag doll Todd's little sister used to carry around.

"You okay?" she asked, her hands on her waist.

"Yeah, sure. Fine," I muttered.

"Didn't mean to scare you," she said.

"I wasn't scared," I lied.

"Really," she said. "I would have been scared, too, if someone grabbed me like that. I really didn't mean to."

"I told you," I said sharply, "I wasn't scared."

"Okay. Sorry."

"What are you sorry about?" I asked. This had to be the weirdest girl I'd ever met.

"I don't know," she replied, shrugging. "I'm just sorry."

"Well, you can stop apologizing," I told her. I brushed the dirt off my clothes and picked up my baseball cap. I quickly set it back on my head. To cover my ears.

The girl stared at me. She stood there and stared. Without saying a word. Was she staring at my ears?

"Who are you?" I finally asked.

"Margaret Ferguson," she replied. "But people call me Fergie. Like the duchess."

I didn't know what duchess she was talking about. But I pretended I did.

"I live through the woods that way," she said, pointing behind her.

"I thought no one lived around here for miles," I said.

"Yeah. There are some houses around here, Cooper," she replied. "They're pretty spread out."

"Hey! How did you know my name?" I asked suspiciously.

Margaret, or Fergie, or whatever her name was, turned beet-red.

"I, uh, watched you move in yesterday," she confessed.

"I didn't see you," I replied.

"That's because I hid in the woods," she said. "I heard your father call you Cooper. And I know your last name, too. It's Holmes. I saw it written on all the boxes in the moving van. And I know you have a brother, Mickey," she added. "He's a jerk."

I laughed. "You got that right!" I exclaimed. "So how long have you lived around here?"

She didn't answer. She kept her eyes on the ground.

"I said, how long have — "

Suddenly, her head jerked up and she gazed into my eyes.

25

"Wh-what's wrong?" I asked when I saw her frightened face.

Her face tightened, as if she were in pain. Her lips trembled.

"Margaret!" I cried. "What? What is it?"

She opened her mouth, but no words came out. She breathed deeply, gulping air. Finally, she clutched my shoulders and shoved her face right up close to mine.

"Dogs," she whispered. Then she let go of me and darted away.

I froze for a moment. Then I chased after her.

She made it to a big tree stump before I caught up. I grabbed hold of the back of her T-shirt and spun her around.

"Margaret, what do you mean 'dogs'?" I asked.

"No! No!" she cried. "Just let me go! Let me go!"

I held her tightly.

"Let me go! Let me go!" she cried again.

"Margaret, what did you mean back there?" I repeated. "This is important. Why did you say 'dogs'?"

"Dogs?" Her eyes grew wide. "I don't remember saying that."

My jaw fell open. "You did!" I insisted. "You looked straight at me and said, 'dogs'! I heard you!"

She shook her head. "No, I don't remember that," she replied thoughtfully.

Now I've met weird kids in my life, but Margaret here takes the cake. She almost makes Mickey seem normal.

Almost.

"Okay," I said, trying to sound calm, "here's what happened. You freaked out. Then you grabbed me. Then you said, 'Dogs.' Then you freaked out again."

"Don't remember," she replied softly, shaking her head from side to side. "Why would I say that?"

"I don't know!" I screamed, starting to lose it. "I'm not the one who said it!"

She gazed around in all directions, then focused those green, crazy eyes on me.

"Listen to me, Cooper," she whispered mysteriously. "Get away from here."

"Huh?"

"I'm warning you, Cooper! Tell your parents they must leave at once!" She glanced nervously behind her, then turned back to me.

"Please — listen to me. Get away from here! As fast as you can!"

# 7

Fergie let go of my shoulders and ran.

For a few seconds, I stared after her, too shocked to move. Then I decided I'd better not let her get away.

"Fergie!" I called out. "Wait up!"

For a girl, Fergie ran pretty fast. Actually, most girls I know are fast runners.

Whoever said they were slower than boys in the first place? It isn't true. Lots of girls in my class last year could beat any guy in a race.

Anyway, *I* happen to be a very fast runner. When you're afraid of everything, you learn to run — fast!

"Fergie!" I called again. "Please! Tell me what's going on!" But I couldn't catch up.

Then, to my surprise, she stopped and turned back to me. "Listen, Cooper," she said, calmer than before. "The woods are haunted. Your house is probably haunted, too. Go home. Go home and tell your parents to move back to wherever you came from."

"But — but — but — " I sputtered.

"It's too dangerous here," Fergie warned. "Get away, Cooper. As fast as you can!"

With that, she turned and walked away in the direction of her house.

I didn't follow her this time.

I should have. I totally forgot that I was lost.

I turned around. My house is probably in the opposite direction, I decided.

She disappeared through the trees. Fine with me, I thought angrily. It would be fine with me if I never saw her again.

Why did she tell me all that?

Why did she say the woods were haunted?

Because it was true?

Leave it to my parents to buy a haunted house in haunted woods!

I continued on, unable to shake the creepy feeling I had. I felt as if a hundred eyes were stalking me through the trees.

I wished Fergie had kept her mouth shut.

The longer I walked, the more frightened I became. Now I was *positive* that the woods were haunted. Haunted by ghosts tracking every step I made.

Then, in the distance, I heard a faint banging. It startled me at first. When I realized it was Dad working on the grill, I shrieked with joy.

"All right! I'm almost home!" My plan had worked.

I followed the hammering sounds.

Something rustled the branches above my head and made me jump.

I gazed up.

Just a bird.

Staring up at the trees, I nearly fell headfirst into a stream.

The water lapped quietly against the grassy shore. It reflected the pale blue morning sky above it.

Funny, I hadn't seen this stream here before.

I bent down to touch the water. Cold.

This is awesome! I thought. A real stream, practically in my own backyard.

Then I remembered that it wouldn't be my backyard for long. As soon as I told my parents what Fergie had said, we'd pack up and move back to Boston.

As I dried my hand on my shirt, I had that creepy feeling again. The feeling of eyes watching me. My head jerked up, and I gasped.

There *were* eyes watching me.

Four dark eyes glared at me from across the stream.

The eyes of two enormous black Labradors.

One dog panted loudly, its tongue hanging out. The other dog flashed its teeth at me. Ugly, yellow teeth.

They both uttered low, menacing growls.

Not friendly. Not friendly at all.

Run! I urged myself. Run!

But my legs wouldn't budge.

Growling, the dogs eyed me hungrily.

Then they attacked.

## 8

Their heavy paws thudded the ground as they came bounding toward me. Their eyes glowed with excitement. Their large heads bobbed up and down.

With a terrified cry, I turned and ran.

If only I could fly!

"Helllllp!" Was that *me* letting out that frightened wail?

Yes. I think it was.

Suddenly, I caught a glimpse of light through the trees. Sunlight glistening off the jungle gym slide!

Yes!

Almost home.

The two black Labs ran at my heels. I could feel their hot breath on the backs of my legs. I felt a pair of sharp teeth scrape my ankle.

With one last gasp of speed, I burst through

the trees and out of the woods. "Dad!" I yelled, racing toward my father.

"Help me!" I shrieked. "The dogs! The dogs!" I threw my arms around his waist and held on.

"Cooper, calm down! What's gotten into you?" my father asked, grabbing me by the shoulders.

"The dogs!" I wailed, refusing to let go of him.

"Cooper, *what* dogs?" Dad demanded.

I blinked at him in confusion. Didn't he hear them? Couldn't he see them?

I let go of him and pointed toward the woods.

"Wild dogs. Big, black Labs, I think. They chased me, and — "

I scanned the yard frantically. Dad and I were alone.

No barking.

No snarling.

The sunlight glistened off the slide.

The tire swung lazily from its rope.

The dogs had vanished.

# 9

"Cooper, this is a joke — right?" Dad asked, shaking his head.

"Huh? No way!" I cried. "They were right behind me. One almost bit me, and — "

"And then they disappeared into thin air!" Dad declared.

"Come into the woods with me," I pleaded. "They've got to be there." I ran to the edge of the woods, desperately searching for some sign of the dogs. Dad followed right behind.

But there was nothing to see.

I turned and slunk back to the house.

Dad didn't say anything until we were back in the yard. He sat down on the jungle gym slide. His eyes studied me.

"Cooper, tell me what's wrong," Dad said in a low voice. I could tell he thought I had made all this up.

"I *told* you, Dad. Two dogs chased me through the woods. They were inches from me! One tried to tear my leg off!"

Dad continued to stare up at me, his expression thoughtful.

"Dad, listen," I pleaded. "We have to move. We can't live here!"

He climbed to his feet. "What are you talking about, Cooper?"

"We have to move back to Boston," I insisted. "We can't stay here!"

"Why not?" Dad asked.

"It's this house!" I shouted, my voice cracking. "It's haunted!"

"Now, Cooper — "

"Dad! Listen to me," I begged. "The woods . . . this house . . . they're all haunted. Everybody around here knows it already! We never should have moved here!"

"Cooper, you're not making any sense," Dad replied, keeping his voice low and calm. "You know, walking in the woods by yourself can be scary. Why don't you come inside and calm down? Mom made a big breakfast. Have some French toast. You'll feel better." He put his arm around my shoulders.

Now I *really* felt upset. My own father didn't believe me.

"But, Dad, it's true!" I insisted. "The woods are haunted, and this weird girl I met warned me to move out! She — "

"Cooper, I know you're unhappy about the move," Dad said. "But these wild stories aren't going to change anything. This is where we live now."

"But — "

"When school starts, you'll make some new friends and everything will be fine. So come on in and have breakfast. You'll feel better. You'll see."

He led me back to the house.

As Dad held the door open for me, I glanced back and took one last look at the woods.

Two big black dogs stared at me from the trees.

## 10

When I blinked, the dogs vanished.

Shaking my head, I made my way into the kitchen.

Mickey had already finished half his breakfast when Dad and I entered the room. He leaned over his cereal bowl, snickering about something. I ignored him.

"Cooper, have some French toast," Mom said. "It's on your plate, waiting for you."

I sat across from Mickey, trying hard not to look at his dumb face. I was still really steamed at him.

"Mom, do you know who our neighbors are?" I asked, pouring maple syrup over the toast.

"Why, sure," Mom answered. "Your father and I met some of them a few weeks ago when we came to see the house."

"Did you meet the Fergusons?" I asked.

Mom squinted her eyes, thinking. Then she

shook her head. "No, I don't think we met them. We met the Martells. Joel and Shirley. Very nice people." Then she asked, "Who are the Fergusons?"

I didn't answer. I pressed on. "Did the Martells tell you our house was haunted?"

Mom laughed. "No, Cooper, they didn't. It must have slipped their minds," she joked.

"Ha-ha. It's nothing to laugh about," I insisted. "Our house *is* haunted. And so are the woods!"

"Cooper, what are you talking about?" my mother demanded.

"Enough, Cooper," my father warned. "Eat your breakfast."

"Yeah," Mickey said with a snort. "Eat your breakfast, Drooper."

I could feel my face turn red. I hated when Mickey called me Drooper. He called me that because of my big droopy ears.

"Shut up, *Sickey*," I replied.

"Cut it out, you two," Dad snapped.

I dug my fork into the French toast. How could they not believe me? Did they really think I made this story up?

I lifted a chunk of toast to my mouth and stuffed it in.

"Aghhhh!"

Choking and coughing, I spit the food out on my plate.

"Gross!" Mickey cried, grinning. "Gross! A guy could lose his appetite around here."

My eyes teared, and I coughed a few more times.

"You okay, Cooper?" Mom asked.

"Somebody dumped salt on my French toast!" I exclaimed angrily.

Mickey started to laugh.

That creep.

My father climbed up from the table. Without saying a word, he stomped out of the room.

That's how my Dad acts when he's angry. He gets all quiet, then just walks away. Punishments come later.

I gulped down a glass of milk, trying to wash the salt out of my mouth. Mom returned to the stove to make another batch of French toast for me.

"Mickey," she said, sighing, "you know that wasn't funny. Now apologize to your brother."

"Apologize? But it was just a joke!" Mickey complained.

"We're all cracking up," I muttered bitterly, gulping down a second glass of milk. "You're a real riot."

"Apologize!" my mother insisted again.

Mickey hung his head and stared at the floor.

I folded my arms across my chest. "I'm waiting!" I sang happily.

Mickey made an ugly face at me. When Mom turned around, he changed his expression to an innocent smile.

"I'm so sorry, Cooper," Mickey oozed. "It won't happen again." He blinked innocently.

Satisfied, Mom turned back to the stove.

As soon as she did, Mickey pulled on his ears, trying to stretch them as big as mine.

I'd had it with Mickey. I pushed my chair away from the table and hurried out of the room. I didn't want to get into another fight with my stupid brother now.

I had more important things to do. I had to talk to Dad about the dogs. I had to make him believe me.

Dad sat in his favorite chair, which just didn't look right in our new living room. Even he seemed to notice. He kept shifting uncomfortably.

"Maybe it's time for a new chair," he muttered.

"Dad, can I talk to you for a second?" I asked.

"What is it, Cooper?" he asked as he moved Great-grandma's lamp closer to the chair.

"It's about the dogs," I said.

Dad sighed. "Really, Cooper. Aren't you making too big a deal about this? So *what* if you saw dogs in the woods? They could belong to anybody!"

"But they chased me!" I replied, getting all

worked up again. "And then they disappeared into thin air! And after that girl told me the woods were haunted — "

"What girl?" my dad demanded.

"She said her name was Margaret Ferguson," I told him. "She said her family lived next door."

Dad rubbed his chin. "That's strange," he said. "The real estate broker never mentioned the Fergusons."

"Well, I met her this morning, and she told me everyone around here knows that our house is haunted!"

"Maybe that's why we got such a good deal on the house," Dad muttered, chuckling.

I didn't see what was so funny.

He stopped laughing and stared at me seriously. "Forget about the dogs for now, Cooper. We'll deal with it if you see them again. In the meantime, I'll ask around in town if anyone knows who owns them. Okay?"

"But what about the house?" I asked. "Margaret said we should move as fast as we can."

"French toast is ready!" Mom called out, interrupting me. "Come on, Cooper. Before it gets cold."

"Go eat," my father urged. "And please. Not another word about dogs or the house being haunted."

With a sigh, I headed back to the kitchen. As I stepped through the door, Mickey jumped in my face and let out a roar.

Naturally, it scared me to death.

"Mom!" I cried.

"Mickey, enough!" my mother screamed. "Stop teasing Cooper. He's having a hard time adjusting to the new house."

"No, I'm not!" I yelled at her. Why wasn't anybody taking me seriously? "This house is haunted. You'll be sorry you didn't listen to me. You'll be sorry!"

Then I stormed out and stomped off to my room. I collapsed on my bed and gazed around. Same old stuff, but the room didn't feel like my own.

I stayed in there all day. I didn't want to see Mickey. I didn't want to see Mom and Dad. And I really didn't want to see those dogs again.

By dinnertime, I'd unpacked most of my things. The room felt a little better. More like my old bedroom back in Boston.

After dinner, I lugged all seventy-seven snow domes into the bathroom and washed them, one by one. People don't realize that you have to take care of snow domes and keep them clean and filled with water or they'll dry out.

When they were all sparkling clean, I arranged them carefully on my new bookcase.

They looked awesome!

I tried to organize them in some sort of size order, but that didn't work. Instead, I alphabetized them — from Annapolis to Washington, D.C. Of course, I placed my absolute favorite dome — a Boston Red Sox snow dome — on the middle shelf, front and center.

I finished at eleven, then got ready for bed. All that unpacking had tired me out.

I had closed my eyes and was just drifting off to sleep when I heard it.

Loud and clear.

Barking.

And growling.

Outside my window.

I bolted straight up in bed.

I waited for my parents and Mickey to come running in. This time, they must have heard the dogs, too.

I waited. And waited.

The barking grew louder.

No one else in the house stirred.

I lowered one foot to the floor, then the other. I stood up, listening hard.

Listening to the two dogs barking.

And to my horror, I realized that this time the barking wasn't outside my window.

This time it was coming from *inside my house!*

# 11

Frantically, I searched for a weapon. Something to protect me from the barking dogs.

I found my aluminum baseball bat in the closet. I gripped it tightly and crept across the room to my bedroom door.

I pushed it open. And listened.

Yes.

The barking was definitely coming from inside the house. From the living room, I decided.

I took a deep breath and slipped into the hallway. Where were my parents? Their bedroom is directly over the living room on the second floor. They had to hear this.

Why hadn't they come running out?

Mickey's room was on the first floor down the hall from mine. I peered down the hall and saw that his bedroom door was closed.

What's his problem? I wondered. Where *is* everyone?

I crept quietly down the hall, inching my way to the living room. I could hear the dogs racing around in there.

I gasped when I heard a loud crash.

Something clattered to the floor. Great-grandma's lamp, I guessed.

I stared up at the ceiling — to my parents' bedroom. Were they deaf or something?

Holding the bat in front of me, I jumped into the living room and snapped on the ceiling light.

The dogs were . . .

The dogs were . . .

NOT THERE!

The room stood empty.

"Huh?" I blinked a few times from the sudden brightness of the light, then stared around the room.

No dogs.

No growling. No barking.

But, wait! Great-grandma's lamp lay on its side on the floor.

I took a step over to the sofa. Something crunched under my bare feet.

Potato chips?

Yes. Potato chips. Scattered across the room.

I spotted the potato chip bag — ripped to shreds on the floor.

My heart thumped so hard, I thought it might burst out of my chest.

As I bent to pick up the torn bag, a shadow fell over me.

I heard heavy breathing.

And I felt a gust of hot, smelly breath shoot across my neck.

# 12

"Drooper, what are you doing?"

I straightened up and spun around.

"Mickey!"

"That's my name. Don't wear it out," he replied.

"Mickey! Did you hear them? Did you?"

Mickey glanced around the room. "Hear who?" he asked. Then, before I could answer, he snapped, "Cooper, you jerk, why did you throw potato chips around the living room?"

"The dogs!" I cried. "The dogs did it! Did you hear them?"

Mickey shook his head. "No way. I didn't hear anything."

I was stunned. "You didn't hear wild dogs running around the room a few minutes ago?"

Mickey rolled his eyes and whistled. "You're losing it, Cooper. Hearing invisible dogs is one thing. But feeding them potato chips? You're really messed up, man."

"I didn't do this!" I said angrily. "I told you. The dogs did."

Mickey shook his head. "Just promise me one thing," he said seriously.

"What?" I asked.

"Promise me when school starts next week, you won't tell anybody you're related to me."

I wanted to throw something at him. I wished I had Great-grandma's lamp in my hand, but I didn't. So I threw what I did have — the empty potato chip bag.

It flew about three inches, then dropped at my feet.

"You're pathetic!" Mickey laughed. "I know why you're doing this, too. You're trying to make Mom and Dad think the house is haunted. So then they'll move back to Boston, and you can see your dweeby little friends Gary and Todd again."

He made a face at me. "Dumb, Drooper. Really dumb."

He shuffled away, shaking his head.

Just you wait, Mickey, I thought. I'm going to get even with you. Just you wait.

And I'm going to make everyone believe me about the dogs. I'm going to make everyone believe that I'm telling the truth.

But how? I wondered, gazing around the empty, silent living room.

How?

# 13

Sunday morning I woke up early as usual. I had only a few more things to unpack, and I knew I could finish before breakfast.

I unrolled my Red Sox poster and tacked it to the wall, over my bed. Same place I'd hung it in Boston.

Then I rummaged through a box, searching for my lucky pair of red socks. As I was slipping them on my feet, I heard the doorbell ring.

"Cooper!" my mother called to me a few seconds later. "There's someone here to see you!"

Who could it be? I didn't know anybody here.

Then I had a thought. Maybe Gary asked his dad to drive him and Todd up to Maine to surprise me!

Wow! What a great surprise!

I closed the box and charged out of my room, down the hall, and to the front door. I was so excited!

But no Gary and Todd.

Fergie stared at me from the front doorway. I could see at first glance that she was kind of nervous. She kept shifting her weight from one foot to the other. And she twirled a lock of her bright red hair between her fingers.

"Oh. Hi," I mumbled, unable to hide my disappointment.

"I need to talk to you," she said. "Right away."

"Okay, sure," I replied.

"Not here," she said, nudging her head toward the den where my mom and dad were reading the newspaper.

I sighed. "Okay, wait a sec." I ran back to my room and pulled on a pair of sneakers.

"Let's go out back," I suggested. She nodded solemnly and followed me outside.

I swung on the tire and listened to Fergie. "It was all your brother's idea!" she blurted out.

"Excuse me?" I cried.

"I don't know why I agreed to do it, but it was really all his idea. Every bit of it."

"What was?" I asked.

"Everything I told you yesterday. About your house. And the woods."

"You mean they're not haunted?" I asked, confused.

Fergie shook her head. "Of course not."

"But why did you tell me they were?" I asked.

"I told you, it was all Mickey's idea. I met Mickey the day you moved in," Fergie explained. "He told me it would be funny if I played this trick on you."

"He *what*?" I cried.

"He told me the two of you always played all kinds of tricks on each other," Fergie replied. "He said you would think it was a riot."

"A joke?" I asked. "It was all one of Mickey's jokes?" I couldn't believe it.

Fergie bit her bottom lip and nodded. "Mickey said to tell you the woods were haunted. He said to tell you the house was haunted, too." Fergie sighed. "So I did it. But when I saw how scared you were, I felt really bad about it. I wished I hadn't listened to your brother."

Mickey. That jerk.

"But how did you know about the dogs?" I asked.

Fergie stared blankly at me. "Dogs? What dogs?"

"That's the word you whispered to me," I explained. "Dogs."

Fergie twisted her face, thinking hard. "No, I don't remember saying that. Are you sure I said 'dogs'?"

I nodded. "Definitely. That was all you said.

51

Dogs. And, then, after you ran off, two mean-looking black Labradors chased me through the woods."

"Really?"

I nodded. "They chased me all the way home. Then they just vanished."

"Weird," Fergie mumbled.

"Tell me about it," I replied, rolling my eyes.

"Where did you first see the dogs?" Fergie asked me.

I pointed into the woods. "Back there. Near a stream."

"That's the stream that leads to the Martells' house," Fergie said. "They're friends of my parents. They don't own any dogs, Cooper."

I shrugged, then batted a fly that buzzed in my ear. "Well, someone around here must have dogs," I told her.

"I'm scared of dogs," Fergie admitted. "I'm glad I didn't see them yesterday."

"They weren't nice dogs," I muttered. "You wouldn't like them."

"Hey, did you see a big rock in the shape of an arrowhead when you were near the stream?" she asked.

I shook my head. "No, I didn't."

"It's really cool," she gushed. "You should check it out. I go there all the time. It's a great rock for climbing."

"Let's check it out now," I suggested. I still thought the woods were scary — haunted or not. But I didn't feel like hanging around the house.

I hopped off the tire and followed Fergie into the woods. I spotted a long, thick stick and picked it up. "In case the dogs come back," I told Fergie.

We walked a little while until we reached the stream. Fergie searched around for her rock.

"I know it's here somewhere," she said, turning to me. "I can never — "

She stopped short when her eyes met mine.

"Cooper!" she whispered. "What is it?"

I stumbled backwards. My hand trembled as I pointed to the trees directly behind Fergie.

"Mar — Margaret!" I whispered in terror. "The dogs! Look out! They're coming! They're coming right at us!"

# 14

Fergie spun around. She let out a frightened cry.

"Here they come!" I shrieked.

Fergie froze in terror. "Oh, no! Help me, Cooper! I told you! I'm afraid of dogs!"

"Run!" I shouted at her. "Run!"

In a flash, Fergie dashed past me. I've never seen anyone run so fast.

She ran about ten steps. Then her hands flew up as she tripped over a rock.

She uttered a shrill cry of panic and went sprawling on the ground.

I had to laugh. "Got you back!" I cried gleefully.

"Huh?" Fergie lifted her head.

"I got you back," I repeated. "For playing that mean trick on me. For helping Mickey."

I watched as the color slowly returned to Fergie's face. "You scared me to death," she muttered. "How could you play such a horrible joke?"

"Easy," I replied, still grinning.

Fergie growled at me. "I told you, it wasn't totally my fault. Your brother said you played tricks on each other all the time." Then she stood up and shook her head. "That was mean, Cooper. Really mean."

I shrugged. "Yeah. I know. But now we're even."

Fergie brushed some dirt off her jeans and examined a scrape on her elbow. "You know, we should both get back at Mickey," she said.

"I've been thinking about that all morning," I told her. "And yesterday, too. Mickey's been playing really mean tricks on me since we moved here. And I have to get back at him. But it has to be something totally awesome."

We walked along the stream a while longer, trying to figure out how to get back at Mickey. Then Fergie found the arrowhead rock.

She climbed up first, and I followed. It was a big, craggy rock, great for climbing.

We hung out on the rock, thinking up ways to get Mickey back. Fergie wanted to drag him deep into the woods blindfolded and leave him stranded. But I didn't think that would scare Mickey one bit.

I jumped off the rock and began circling it. Sometimes I think better on my feet.

On my third trip around, I got my foot caught in a thick, leafy plant. I glanced down — and cried out. "Oh, perfect! I'm standing in poison ivy!"

Fergie laughed. "It only looks like poison ivy," she assured me. "My science teacher checked it out last year. She told us it's a harmless weed."

I smiled a really evil smile.

"I think I have a great idea. What if we pulled out a bunch of this stuff? What if it somehow ended up in Mickey's bed? Would he freak — or what?"

"He might," Fergie agreed, grinning down at me.

We gathered a bunch of the weeds. They grew all along the stream. So we picked some more as we walked slowly back to my house.

Just past the stream, Fergie showed me a clearing in the trees I hadn't noticed before. A small clearing filled with wildflowers.

I knew right away Mom would flip out if she saw them. She always bought flowers at the Faneuil Hall market back in Boston. I started to pick some for her.

I reached down for a few pretty violet and yellow flowers when something moving through the trees caught my eye. I glanced up just in time to see Mickey stagger into the clearing.

Fergie and I both cried out when we spotted him.

Mickey's clothes were ripped and shredded.

Dark scratches covered his face and arms. And bright red blood trickled down his neck.

"Cooper," he croaked weakly, barely able to talk. "Cooper — the dogs — "

Those were the last words he spoke before he crumpled to the ground.

# 15

"Mickey!" I screamed in horror.

I dropped the wildflowers and weeds and ran to his side.

Fergie and I knelt down beside him. "Is he okay?" she asked, her voice barely above a whisper.

I leaned over him and, with both hands, tugged on his tattered shirt. But I couldn't pull him up. With each try, his limp body slumped back to the ground.

"Mickey! Mickey!" I cried his name again and again. "Are you all right? The dogs! Did they — ?"

As I leaned in closer, Mickey's arms shot up and clamped around my neck. He yanked me to the ground. Then he jumped up and sat on top of me.

He was giggling like an idiot.

"Oh, Mickey! Mickey!" he shrieked in a high voice. "Mickey! Are you all right?"

I started to sputter, but no words came out.

"What a wimp!" he teased. "Do you have to fall for the fake blood every single time?" He let out another long, high-pitched giggle.

I shut my eyes and prayed that I'd disappear. I couldn't believe my brother had tricked me again. In front of Fergie.

My face grew hot. "I'll pound you for this!" I shouted, struggling to push him off me.

"Ooooh! I'm shaking!" Mickey snorted.

"Don't you have anything better to do than to try and scare me?" I yelled.

"I don't even have to try," Mickey replied, grinning.

Fergie stood over us, her arms crossed in front of her.

"Were you in on this little joke, too?" I demanded angrily.

"No! No way!" Fergie insisted.

Mickey pinned my arms to the ground. "Say 'Uncle,' wimp."

I'd never been so embarrassed in my life. Never.

And that includes the time Mickey locked me out of the house in my underwear.

"You're dead meat!" I shouted in his face.

"What are you going to do, Drooper? Knock me out with your bouquet of violets?"

He threw his head back and laughed at his stupid joke. Lucky for me, it gave me a chance to bite his arm.

"Ow! You *mutant*! Look what you did! I'm bleeding!"

He jumped up and examined the bite mark on his arm. Then he growled at me, turned, and trotted away.

I wanted to chase after him. But Margaret held me back.

"Let him go," she said, clutching my shirt. "He's a creep. Really."

Grumbling to myself, I brushed off my clothes. Then I picked up the flowers for Mom. I couldn't face Fergie.

"Are you going home?" she asked.

"Uh-huh," I grunted.

"Will I see you in school tomorrow?"

I shrugged. I wished she would leave me alone. I wanted to be by myself.

I grunted again. I think she got the message.

"Well, guess I'll head home now. Don't worry, Cooper," she said, starting in the direction of her house. "We'll come up with a plan to get him back. I promise."

I didn't answer.

"See you tomorrow!" she called out, waving.

I didn't bother to wave back. I watched her leave. Then I made my way over to the stream to take a drink of cold water. The sight of Mickey all bloody had made my throat dry. And it was from screaming.

I leaned over the sparkling, cool water and lowered my hand. I scooped some water up to my mouth and drank.

But when I saw my reflection in the stream, I choked.

It wasn't me.

The face staring back at me in the water was the face of a black dog!

I jerked my head up.

No dogs on the shore.

No dogs anywhere in sight.

"Whoa!" I cried aloud.

I leaned over the stream again and peered into the water.

The dog stared up at me from beneath the surface.

I raised my head again. No dog on the shore.

So how could I see a dog's reflection in the water?

Once again, I squinted into the clear stream. The dog appeared to ripple with the water.

And as I gaped at the eerie reflection in horror, it pulled back its thin lips and bared its ugly yellow teeth in a silent growl.

# 16

I raced home without glancing back.

I crashed through the front door and charged straight for the bathroom. I had to check myself out in the mirror.

I don't know what I thought I'd see.

A dog face staring back at me?

Even I know how stupid that sounds.

But I couldn't explain the dog reflection in the water. I should have seen *my* face in that stream — not the growling face of a black Lab.

Stepping into the bathroom, I approached the mirror slowly. I peeked in.

And I saw — my own freckled face.

Did it make me feel better?

Not much.

I didn't speak to anyone in my family for the rest of the afternoon. And at dinnertime, I nibbled a few bites, then asked to be excused.

"Are you feeling okay, Cooper?" Mom asked, frowning. "Liver and onions is your favorite. I've never seen you leave liver and onions on your plate."

She walked over and felt my forehead. That's what she always does whenever I act a little strange. Feels my forehead.

"I'm fine, Mom," I replied. "I'm just not very hungry. That's all."

"Cooper is probably a little nervous about tomorrow. His first day in a new school," Dad said to Mom. He turned to me. "Am I right?"

"Yeah, that's it," I agreed. No sense in bringing up the dogs again. No one would believe me, anyway.

"Aw. Poor little Drooper. Scared of his new school," Mickey teased.

Mom and Dad shot Mickey a warning glance. "Mickey — not tonight," Dad muttered.

I ignored my dumb brother. I climbed up from my chair and headed for my room.

I couldn't fall asleep that night. Every time I closed my eyes, I saw the face of the angry black dog, rippling in the stream.

I finally dozed off after midnight.

I awoke to Mom's impatient cries. "Cooper. Cooper. You've overslept. Time to get up!"

I couldn't believe it. I'm always up early. I never oversleep.

I'm going to be late for my first day of school! I thought unhappily. And it's all because of those creepy dogs.

I threw my T-shirt and jeans on and rushed down the hall to the kitchen. No time for a big breakfast. I gulped down a glass of milk. Then I opened the fridge and reached for the peanut butter and jelly to make a sandwich for lunch.

As I spread the peanut butter on the bread, I heard whimpering behind me.

"Cut it out, Mickey," I said without turning around.

The whimpering grew louder.

"Mickey! Quit it! Stop being such a — "

They sprang out of nowhere. The dogs.

They were *in the kitchen*!

# 17

Their jaws hung loose. They drooled hungrily. Thick yellow drool.

My knees buckled. I clutched for the counter to steady myself.

Their dark, furry bodies shimmered under the bright kitchen lights. Growling, their teeth bared, they stepped side by side away from the wall.

I moved back slowly. One small step.

Their dark eyes tracked my move.

One more step back. Slowly. Then another.

Their steady gaze followed me.

The back door stood inches away. If I reached back, I could touch the doorknob now.

I reached back. Slowly. Very slowly.

My hand fumbled. Then I found it. The small round knob . . .

Too late!

They jumped.

I screamed as their dark bodies hurtled toward me.

I shut my eyes.

I heard the sound of snapping jaws.

I opened my eyes in time to see one of the dogs snatch my lunch from the counter.

Then they disappeared.

*Through* the kitchen door. They dove right *through* the wooden door.

Breathing hard, I sank into a kitchen chair.

I held my head tightly. I shut my eyes and tried to calm myself.

I had just seen two dogs run right through a door. How could that be?

Mom raced into the room. Dad followed.

"Cooper, what's wrong?" Mom cried. "What was that horrible scream we heard?"

I had to tell them what happened. I had to. This was too weird. Too scary and too weird.

So I told them the whole story.

"Two black dogs — they jumped through the wall. Into the kitchen. One of them grabbed my lunch. Then they dove through the door."

Big mistake.

Mom and Dad gave me a lecture about the stress of moving. I think I heard them mention the word *psychiatrist*.

They didn't believe a word of it.

I didn't have the strength to argue. I shuffled out the door and headed for school.

No way I could stop thinking about those dogs. Dogs that only I could see. Dogs that stole lunches. Dogs that could walk through doors.

I didn't see them again that week. But every morning I'd hear them barking somewhere around the house. Nobody else heard them.

On Friday, I met Fergie after school and we walked home together. She talked nonstop about our math teacher, but I wasn't really paying attention. I couldn't stop thinking about the dogs.

"What?" I asked Fergie. She'd just asked me something about math homework.

"I *said*," she repeated impatiently, "that we can do our math homework together this weekend."

I shrugged. "Yeah, whatever."

Fergie was going to stay at our house Saturday night. Her parents had to go to Vermont for the weekend.

We had become pretty good friends this past week. So had our parents. Mom and Dad invited the Fergusons over for dinner on Tuesday, and the Fergusons had us over on Wednesday.

Maybe having Fergie sleep over will be fun, I

thought. If I can shut those dogs out of my mind.

"We still have to come up with a trick to play on Mickey," Fergie pointed out. "I've been thinking — "

"Listen, Fergie," I said, interrupting her. "There's something I've been meaning to tell you all week."

She waited for me to begin.

I took a deep breath, then blurted out the whole story. About the dog reflection in the stream. And the dogs in the kitchen.

"I've been hearing them all week," I confessed. "Sometimes outside the house, sometimes inside. It's been a nightmare."

Fergie's jaw dropped open. "How come you didn't tell me before?" she asked.

I sighed. "Because no one in my family believes me," I said. "I thought you wouldn't, either."

"I believe you, Cooper," she replied solemnly.

I smiled. "Thanks, Fergie. That means a lot."

Fergie's expression turned thoughtful. "Well, maybe we'll both hear them on Saturday night. Your parents will have to believe *both* of us."

I nodded. Fergie was right. Mom and Dad couldn't think the *two* of us needed to see a doctor. I started to feel a little more cheerful.

"Now about the get-back-at-Mickey plan," Fergie said. "I have another idea."

I tried to listen to Fergie's plan — it had something to do with rats and a rope — but I couldn't concentrate on what she was saying. I could only think about the dogs.

Would they turn up again this weekend?

# 18

I watched each minute tick away on the alarm clock near my bed. Finally — midnight. Time to get moving.

I tiptoed down the hall to the guest room where Fergie slept. I knocked on the door.

"Fergie," I whispered. "Fergie, get up!"

She appeared at the door in an instant, fully dressed. "The dogs? Are the dogs here?" she asked, eyes wide with fright.

She seemed really spooked. And she had awful pillow-hair static.

"No, dope." I whispered. "It's time to scare Mickey."

Fergie rubbed her eyes. "Oh, yeah, right."

Without saying another word, she slid under the bed and came out with a shoe box and some string.

"Let me see it again," I said eagerly.

Fergie smiled, then opened the box. Inside sat

a huge, hairy, totally gross, disgusting black rat.

A fake, of course. But it looked *so* real! Real enough to fool another rat. A rat like Mickey.

I lifted the rat from the box and shook it in Fergie's face.

She backed away and let out a yelp, even though she knew it was made of rubber or something.

I tied the string around the rat's neck and waved at Fergie to follow me. We crept silently into the hall and headed for Mickey's room.

This was going to be totally awesome! I couldn't wait to see the look on Mickey's face when our hairy rat slithered across his bed!

We stopped in the hall outside Mickey's room. His door stood slightly open. I poked my head in and checked out his bedroom.

By the dim light in the hallway, I could see Mickey in bed, all covered up, fast asleep. Mickey never sleeps with a pillow. He always tosses it on the floor when he climbs into bed. There it was, next to his shoes.

I stepped back from the door and pulled Fergie aside.

"Okay, here's the plan," I whispered. "When we're inside the room, go to the left. That's where the closet is. I'll tiptoe over to the bed and put the rat on Mickey. Then I'll meet you in the closet."

"Check," Fergie whispered solemnly.

"And, remember," I warned her, "be quiet!"

"Check," Fergie said again.

With the rat in one hand, I carefully made my way into Mickey's room. I glimpsed Fergie heading left to the closet. I headed right.

I had nearly reached Mickey's bed when I heard a loud *crack*.

My heart jumped to my throat. I spun around and stared at Fergie in horror.

I saw instantly what had happened. She had stepped on Mickey's skateboard.

We both turned to the bed.

Mickey didn't move a muscle.

He hadn't heard the noise.

I let out a quiet sigh of relief, then shot Fergie a warning glance.

She nodded nervously.

I watched as she opened the closet door and ducked inside.

I held the rat out in front of me and edged closer to Mickey's bed. My hand shook, but I gripped the hairy creature tightly.

I stared down at Mickey under the covers. He slept soundly.

I crept closer.

Bundled under the blankets, it was impossible to tell where Mickey's body started. I set the rat down gently, near his stomach, I think.

Then I tiptoed to the closet. Inside, I knelt next to Fergie and gave her a thumbs-up sign.

Operation "Scare Mickey" was in effect.

And I couldn't be more excited.

It served him right.

I quietly pulled the closet door toward me, leaving it open just a crack. I held tightly onto the end of the string.

"Ready?" I whispered.

"Ready," she whispered back.

"Okay," I said. "On three. One . . . two . . . uh, Fergie, stop kicking me."

"I'm not touching you," she whispered sharply.

"You are, too. Stop it, okay?"

"No way. My feet are all the way over here," Fergie protested.

"Ow! You kicked me again!" I whispered.

She raised her voice. "I did not!"

I clamped my hand over her mouth.

We both froze.

I heard breathing.

Heavy breathing.

Not my breathing. Not Fergie's breathing.

I swallowed hard.

"F-Fergie," I stammered. "We're not alone in here!"

# 19

A low, steady growl proved me right.

Someone — or *something* — was hiding in the closet with us.

We listened to the low growls for another second or two.

Then we both flew out of the closet, screaming in horror.

I only made it a few feet. I tripped over Mickey's skateboard. Went sprawling headfirst. Landed flat on my face.

As I struggled to my feet, I saw a dark figure step out of the closet.

"You!" I screamed in a hoarse, frightened voice.

Mickey grinned back at Fergie and me. "Oooohhh! Oooooooohhh! Look at me!" he cried. "I'm a killer poodle!"

Fergie and I stared at him in disbelief. He had been in the closet the entire time.

I dove to the bed and pulled down the blanket.

"Oh, wow!" I cried out when I saw a bunch of rolled up sheets and towels.

"But how did you know?" Fergie asked him. "How did you know we were coming?"

Mickey flashed us both a smug smirk. "When you showed up this morning clutching that dumb box and whispering to Cooper, I knew something was up. I've been spying on you two jerks all day."

"You sneak!" I cried.

"A sneak? Me?" Mickey replied innocently. "What do you call what you're doing, prowling around my room and hiding in my closet?"

I was so angry. So disappointed. Our great revenge plan — totally ruined.

I grabbed Fergie by the arm. "Come on. Let's get out of here."

"That's right!" Mickey called gleefully after us. "Running away with your tails between your legs!" Then he howled and barked some more.

Great guy — huh?

Fergie and I sat in the hall outside my room. We had really wanted to give Mickey a good scare. So he could see how it felt.

But we had messed up. Totally.

"We'll get him next time," Fergie offered. "We'll come up with an even better plan. Maybe something with knives and fake blood."

I shrugged. I didn't want to wait. I wanted to scare Mickey out of his skin — *tonight*!

Not much chance of that.

Fergie and I yawned at the same time. Then we both stood up. "Guess we should go back to bed. Maybe — "

"Did you hear that?" I asked, cutting Fergie off.

She nodded. "Yeah. I hear it. Barking."

"That's not my brother," I whispered. "It's definitely the dogs!"

# 20

"I don't get it!" Fergie cried in a trembling voice. "Where are your parents? Where's Mickey?"

I led her down the hall, in the direction of the barking.

"I told you," I whispered. "They can't hear the dogs. I don't know why. No one can hear them but us!"

We turned into the living room and gasped.

Two sets of red eyes glowed in the dark.

I reached for Great-grandma's lamp, but knocked it over. It crashed loudly to the floor.

The dogs barked.

Fergie clutched my shoulder. Her hand trembled. "Turn on the lights! Please!" she pleaded.

But before I could reach the switch, the lights snapped on.

We spun around. And there stood Mom on the stairway, glaring down at us. "Cooper! Margaret! What on earth are you two doing?"

"It's the dogs, Mom!" I cried. "See? They're — "

"What dogs?" Mom called.

I spun around.

No glaring red eyes. No dogs. Except for Fergie and me, the room stood empty.

"Wow, your mom sure was upset," Fergie whispered as we trudged back down the hall to our rooms.

"But now you believe me, right, Fergie?" I asked. "You heard the dogs yourself!"

Fergie nodded. "For sure. There were definitely dogs here."

"Go to sleep!" Mom called sternly. "Immediately!"

"Okay, Mom!" I called back. I turned to Fergie. "We'll check out the woods in the morning," I told her. "Those dogs have to be somewhere!"

"Good idea," Fergie agreed. "See you in the morning."

Back in my room, I couldn't fall asleep. I sat on my bed and tossed a baseball into the air. I watched the numbers slowly click by on my alarm clock.

I thought about the dogs. They were definitely here tonight. Fergie had heard them, too.

But how do they get in and out of my house? I wondered.

And how do they vanish into thin air like that?

And why do they keep bothering *me*? Why?

I tossed down the baseball and crept into the hall.

I knocked softly on Fergie's door. "It's me. Can I come in?"

"What's wrong?" she whispered, opening the door.

"Listen," I said. "I don't think I can wait until tomorrow. Let's search for those dogs *now*."

Fergie narrowed her eyes thoughtfully. "It — it might be dangerous," she stammered.

"I don't care," I told her. "Let's go."

# 21

A few minutes later, Fergie and I skulked around the backyard with our flashlights.

No moon tonight. No stars. A chilly mist hung in the air.

We both shivered.

I pointed my flashlight at the ground and searched for paw prints.

None. As usual.

"How come they never leave prints?" I muttered under my breath.

Fergie shrugged, but didn't answer. I could tell she was as scared as I was. She stuck close by my side.

The beam of my flashlight fell on the jungle gym. As I stared down at the ground ahead of me, something suddenly grabbed my ankle.

"Hey!" I yelled, tumbling in the dirt.

I twisted and squirmed, trying to break free. "Help!"

Fergie rushed over to help. Why was she laughing?

"What a klutz! You're all tangled up in the lawn sprinkler!" she exclaimed.

"It's not funny," I insisted. I was glad she couldn't see me blush in the darkness. "I could have broken my leg or something!"

Fergie bent down to help free me. Then she stopped. "Did you hear that?" she asked.

"Hear what?"

"Listen."

We waited silently in the dark. Hardly breathing.

Then I heard it, too. A soft creaking coming from the house. It sounded like an old door swinging open and shut.

We carefully made our way toward the sound. To my surprise, we found a small window low to the ground. I'd never noticed it before.

The window was open, swinging back and forth, making the creaking noise.

"It leads to the basement," I said, poking my head in. "Do you think this is how the dogs get into the house?"

Fergie didn't answer me.

"Fergie?" I called.

No reply.

A chill of fear shot down my back.

I spun around.

In time to see a dark form come charging at me.

Startled, I stumbled. The back of my head hit the house with a hard *thwack*.

The dark creature leaped on top of me.

Pinned me to the ground.

A sour smell filled my nostrils as I struggled to get up.

But I couldn't move.

The creature panted. Its jaws opened wide. Hot saliva dripped on to my face.

The big dog held me prisoner.

What did it plan to do next?

# 22

"Get off me!" I choked out.

I reached up both hands — and shoved with all my might.

To my surprise, the big dog toppled off.

I jumped to my feet, my heart pounding. Spinning around, I saw Fergie. Trapped. Backed up against the house by the other dog.

"Go home!" she cried meekly to the dog. "Go home!"

The dog didn't budge.

I picked up a stick. I waved it furiously in front of me to keep the dogs a good distance away.

As I approached the animals, Fergie shook her arms wildly at them.

They lowered their heads and growled softly.

Then, one of them came running at me. The stick didn't seem to bother him at all.

I lost my balance and crashed into Fergie.

Both dogs curled their lips into fierce, ugly snarls.

My legs were shaking so hard, I could barely stand.

Growling and snapping their jaws, the dogs backed Fergie and me against the house.

"Now what?" Fergie cried, grabbing my arm.

"G-good question," I stammered as the dogs lowered their heads and moved closer.

# 23

I shut my eyes.

I had this crazy idea that if I made them disappear, I'd disappear, too.

Guess what? It didn't work.

I felt a sudden burst of hot, sour dog breath on my face.

Then I felt tugging. On my sweatpants.

I opened my eyes. The dog pulled furiously at my sweats. Not biting. Tugging.

Fergie appeared as confused as I was. The other dog tugged at the hem of her T-shirt.

"What do they want?" Fergie whispered.

"I . . . I . . . I don't know," I answered. "They — they're not biting or attacking!"

"Cooper, I think they want us to go with them," Fergie said.

"That's crazy!" I cried. The dog tugged harder on my sweatpants. "I saw this on a *Lassie* show once!"

"I don't think it's crazy, Cooper," Fergie said. "Watch." She stepped forward slowly, and the dog's tail began to wag. "See? They want us to go with them!"

I hesitated. It seemed ridiculous.

But when I edged forward, the dog that had been tugging on my pants began wagging his tail, too.

"See?" Fergie whispered.

Sorry, but I wasn't buying it. I turned and started to run.

"Cooper, don't!" Fergie cried.

Too late.

The big creature took off after me. Leaped high. And knocked me to the ground.

When I climbed to my feet, he started tugging again.

"Come on. Let's see what they want," Fergie pleaded with me. "We don't have much of a choice, anyway. They're not going to leave us alone."

We followed the dogs through the woods. They stayed close by, never getting too far ahead. And always glancing back.

I pointed my flashlight along the path. The dim light didn't help very much at all. I had no idea where we were going. All I knew was that it was very dark out — and we were headed deeper and deeper into the woods.

"I hope we can find our way *back*," I muttered to myself.

Then, without warning, the dogs sped up. Their big paws trod heavily on the soft ground.

A few seconds later, they began barking and scratching wildly at something between the trees.

I lifted my flashlight and aimed it in their direction.

In the center of a small clearing stood a broken-down wooden shack. The dogs clawed at the door. When they had pushed it open, they came back for us. They began tugging again, pulling us toward the shack.

"Wha — what is this place?" I cried. "Where are we?"

"I don't know," Fergie whispered. "I've never seen this shack before."

The dogs tugged — furiously now. They really wanted us to go in there.

"What can be inside?" I whispered to Fergie.

Fergie swallowed hard. "I don't know," she whispered back. "But I think we're going to find out!"

# 24

"Fergie, I don't like this," I whispered. "Let's get away from here — fast!"

I felt the dog clamp its jaw tighter on my ankle.

Had he understood what I'd said?

"They're not going to let us get away," Fergie said softly.

Snarling and growling, the dogs backed us up against the door to the shack.

"Whoa!" I cried out as the dogs leaped at the side of the shack.

"I don't *believe* it!" Fergie screamed.

The dogs jumped right through the wooden wall. They disappeared inside.

"That's *impossible*!" Fergie cried.

"Tell that to the dogs," I murmured.

I had seen them do it before — in my own kitchen.

"They're *ghosts* or something!" Fergie cried.

I grabbed her arm. "Let's get out of here! Whatever happens . . . we can't go in that shack!"

We'd taken only a few steps when the dogs came tearing out through the shack wall.

They edged in close, pressing us up against the shack again. Before we could struggle or try to get away, the dogs rose up on their hind legs.

Standing up, they were taller than us! Fergie and I exchanged terrified glances.

The dogs staggered forward. Pressed their front paws against our chests. And shoved us backwards into the shack.

We screamed as we started to fall.

The shack had no floor.

We fell, hurtling down. Tumbling as we fell.

Down, down, down.

Into a deep, black hole.

A deep, black hole that didn't seem to end.

# 25

I landed softly on my feet. I didn't even feel it.

Had we fallen into some kind of well? Or a tunnel dug deep under the shack?

I couldn't tell.

I took a deep breath and gazed around the heavy blackness. "Fergie — are you okay?" I called. My voice came out tiny and shrill.

"I — I guess," she replied after a few seconds. "Cooper — *look!*"

I started to reply that it was too dark to see anything. But then I glimpsed the two pairs of red eyes, glaring at us through the darkness.

I gasped.

*"Don't move!"* instructed a dry whisper of a voice.

"Who are you?" I managed to choke out. "What do you want?"

"Why did you dogs bring us here?" Fergie demanded.

"We are not dogs," the voice growled. "We are people."

"But — but — " I sputtered.

"Silence!" the voice commanded. "Silence while you are in the Changing Room."

"The *what*?" I cried.

The red eyes flared.

"Centuries ago, my friend and I had an evil spell cast upon us," the voice continued, ignoring my question. "The spell forced us to roam these woods as dogs. Ghost dogs."

"Too bad," I muttered. "But what do you want *us* for?"

The dogs snickered. It sounded more like dry coughing than laughter.

"You are in the Changing Room," the voice told us. "For nearly a hundred years, we have tried to get two people in here. And now we have succeeded."

"And — ?" I demanded.

"We're going to change places with you," the voice said casually.

"Excuse me?" Fergie cried. "You're going to *what*?"

"We will take your places," the voice repeated. "And you shall take ours. You will be the ghost dogs. You will roam these woods as we did — forever!"

"No way!" I cried. I wanted to run.

But where?

I was surrounded by heavy blackness on all sides.

"Fergie — " I started.

But I heard her gasp. And then I began to feel warm. As if someone had covered me with a heavy blanket.

The warmth swept over my body.

Simmering heat. As if I were in an oven.

Warmer. Warmer. Until sweat dripped down my face, and I was panting in the heat.

I can't stand it anymore! I thought. I'm going to *melt*!

I opened my mouth to scream. But the sounds that escaped my throat weren't mine.

In fact, they didn't sound human at all.

# 26

I opened my eyes to bright sunshine.

The woods around me appeared fuzzy. I struggled to focus.

I yawned. Then I stretched my entire body and shook myself awake.

Yes! That stretch felt good.

I sniffed the air and shook myself again. Wow! Something smelled delicious.

My stomach growled. I suddenly realized I must be starving.

Still trying to focus, I took two steps and fell on my face.

I stood again, feeling unsteady. What's wrong? I wondered.

I gazed around the woods. Why were the trees suddenly all black and white? Why was the sky gray? The grass gray?

What had happened to all the color?

Was this a dream?

I heard a gruff sound behind me. Someone clearing his throat.

I turned — and saw a black Labrador.

I started to cry out — but hoarse barks escaped my throat.

Startled, I glanced down at my own body. My own fur-covered body. "Ohhhh." I dug my front paws into the dirt. I shook myself hard, trying to shake the dog body off. Trying to shake it away so I could see my real body. Cooper's body.

And as I shook, I jerked my head back. And saw a long, black tail!

My tail!

I let out a startled *yip*. I'm a dog, too, I realized.

The ghosts in the Changing Room weren't kidding around. They changed places with us. Fergie and I are dogs.

Fergie whimpered.

Trembling, we both began to trot, our tails hanging between our legs. Fergie's whimpers turned into mournful howls.

What was that? Strange! I thought Fergie said something.

"I *did* say something," she insisted. "Well, actually, I *thought* something. I think we can read each other's thoughts, Cooper."

*Okay, Fergie, then what am I thinking now?*

"You're thinking of that leftover fried liver from

last night that your mom put in the fridge," Fergie thought.

That's right!

We could read each other's mind! Cool!

I licked my lips a few times, thinking about the liver. I loved liver so much, Mom made it for me once a week. Man, did I want that liver now!

Then I remembered I had other things to worry about.

"Fergie, what are we going to do? We're dogs!"

"I can see that, Cooper," she replied, swatting a fly from behind her floppy, black ear.

"Well, we've got to do something!" I cried. "We can't trot around like this forever. Those ghost dogs stole our bodies! They're probably fooling my parents this very minute!"

Fergie didn't reply. Instead, she ran around in circles, chasing her tail. "Hey! This is fun!"

"Fergie! Quit messing around! We're in major trouble!"

"Okay, okay! I'm sorry! I'm upset about this, too, you know!"

Fergie dropped to the dirt. She buried her snout in her front paws. Deep in thought. "You know what, Cooper?"

"What?" I asked as I paced back and forth, trying to think of a way to get us out of this mess.

"Your droopy ears look pretty good — now that you're a dog."

"Fergie! Get serious!" I growled.

Then it hit me.

"I know!" I cried. "I know what we can do. We have to drag those ghosts back to the shack and trade places with them again!"

"Oh, sure, Cooper. No problem," Fergie barked. "And how do you suppose we do that? Walk up to them and say, 'Uh, excuse me, but can you come back to the shack with us? It'll only be for a second.' "

I stared at Fergie. She had become a dog. But her personality hadn't changed one bit!

"I heard that," she mumbled.

I sighed. "Well, do you have a better plan?" I asked, scratching furiously at my neck.

"I'm thinking, I'm thinking," Fergie answered with a yawn. "I'm really so tired. Maybe after a nap — "

"No! No naps! We have to do something — now! Listen to me. We'll get my parents to help. All we have to do is convince them that we're the real Cooper and Margaret, and that those kids in the house are imposters."

"And how are we going to do that?" Fergie asked.

Good question. Real good question.

# 27

Fergie and I trotted through the woods. I sniffed the ground. Sniffed the weeds. So many great smells!

We stopped at the edge of the woods behind my house. I heard laughing, shouting voices. Then I saw my parents. In the backyard. Throwing a Frisbee around with Fergie and Cooper!

Those fakes!

I growled with anger.

I bared my teeth. Prepared to attack.

"Whoa!" Fergie cried. "Cooper, wait! You can't just barge over there and attack them!"

Fergie was right. That wouldn't solve anything.

I watched my dad send the Frisbee flying across the yard.

I had a strong urge to jump up and go for that Frisbee.

But I stopped myself. This was no time for playing.

Then I had an idea. The greatest idea. The idea of a lifetime.

"Come on!" I urged Fergie. I began loping toward the side of my house.

"Cooper, where are you going?" she asked.

I didn't answer. I stopped outside the wall to Mickey's room. "This will just take a second," I told Fergie.

She read my mind. She knew what I planned to do.

Side by side, we leaped through the wall of the house.

And burst into Mickey's room.

He was standing in his underwear. Leaning over his dresser, sorting out his T-shirts. He cried out and spun around as Fergie and I started to growl.

My brother uttered a short, terrified whimper. He started backing up, his eyes wide with fright.

Fergie and I began barking and jumping up on our hind legs.

"How — how did you — ?" Mickey stammered. Those were the only words he could choke out.

Then he let out another whimper, stumbled past us, and bolted out through the bedroom door. "Mommy! Daddy! Help!" I heard him scream. "Mommy! Daddy!"

Fergie and I didn't want to miss seeing him run

through the yard in his underwear. We trotted through the wall and watched until he disappeared around the garage.

"Did you see his face?" I yelped happily. "Was that awesome?!"

"Man, that was excellent!" Fergie cheered.

"Hey, you two!" a stern voice called.

I turned around.

Dad!

"How did you dogs get in this yard?" my father demanded sharply. "Come on. Out! Out!"

"But, wait! Dad! It's me, Cooper!" I tried to yell. But all that came out was *Woof! Woof! Woof!*

"Out! Out!" Dad repeated angrily.

"Dad! Wait! It's really me! Listen! You've got to listen!"

*"Woof! Woof! Woof, woof, woof! Woof! Woof, woof, woof, woof!"*

My father armed himself with a broom and waved it wildly at Fergie and me. "Out!" he cried, shaking the broom at us.

"What's going on?" Mom called from the doorway.

"Mom! It's me. Cooper!" I barked furiously.

"Oh, Sam. Please get rid of those animals! You know I'm allergic to dogs!"

"But, Mom!" I cried. "Can't you tell it's me?"

*Woof, woof! Woof, woof, woof, woof, woof!*

"Please, Sam! Call the pound! These dogs look dangerous. They might have to be put to sleep! Call the pound. They'll know what to do."

I watched in horror as my dad picked up the phone and dialed.

# 28

Fergie and I bolted into the woods as fast as we could. Even as a dog, Fergie ran faster than I did.

We hid among the trees and watched my parents and the fake Cooper and Fergie toss the Frisbee around in the backyard.

The guys from the pound never showed up. But things still looked pretty bad. My parents thought we were stray dogs. And I couldn't tell them who I was.

All I could do was bark.

Hey. Wait a minute. Maybe I could do more than bark.

"Fergie, I have another idea!" I said, wagging my tail. "Follow me!"

Fergie and I sneaked around the side of the house and stepped through the wall into the living room. I sniffed around, searching for a pen and some paper.

"I'll write them a note," I explained to Fergie. "Mom will definitely recognize my handwriting."

I found a pen lying on the coffee table, next to some notepaper.

I tried to lift the pen.

It slipped out from under my paw. I couldn't wrap my paw around it.

Fergie tried to help me. She nosed the pen in my direction, but I still couldn't pick it up.

Impossible. Dogs can't hold pens.

I felt so disappointed. I pushed the pen away, then ripped the paper to shreds. That's when my dad burst in.

"Hey! I thought I told you two dogs to beat it!" my father yelled.

My mother and the two phonies came running into the room.

I started barking, trying to communicate with Dad. But that seemed to annoy him even more.

"Stand up on your hind legs!" I instructed Fergie. "Maybe he'll think we're trying to tell him something!"

I hopped up, trying to balance on my back legs. But I wasn't very good at it. I mean, give me a break. I'd only been a dog for a few hours.

I toppled over onto my stomach.

I must have looked pretty stupid, because everyone started laughing. "Weird dogs," the Cooper imposter said.

Fergie and I hopped up again and again. But nobody understood what we were doing. And after a while, they grew bored with our little act. Dad picked up the broom again.

I probably could have yanked that stupid broom right out of his hands and pinned him to the ground. But what would that prove?

Dad chased Fergie and me out the back door and into the woods.

"You're right," I told her when we were safely hidden by the trees. "We're going to be dogs for the rest of our lives. And not even real dogs. *Ghost* dogs."

"Don't worry, Cooper," Fergie replied, reading my mind. "We'll convince them. There's got to be a way to show them who we are."

I sighed, then rolled on to my back.

If only Gary and Todd were here. They'd know what to do.

I rolled back again. And, suddenly, I felt hot. Burning hot. I sprang up on all fours.

"What is it?" Fergie cried out. "What's wrong?"

I shook violently from head to tail. Out of control. I couldn't stop shaking. Something had taken over my body.

# 29

"Fleas!" I shrieked.

There must have been *thousands* of them! Clinging all over my body! And I couldn't reach them.

"My back!" I cried helplessly. "My back!"

Fergie lifted her front paws and scratched the part of my back I couldn't reach.

"Higher," I pleaded. "Higher. Aaaaahhhhh, that's it!"

My ears drooped low, and I sighed with relief.

Fergie found us a nice spot under a tall birch tree. I stretched out my body and rested my face on my paws. Fergie curled up into a tight ball. It was time to think up another plan.

And time to nap. I couldn't believe how tired I'd suddenly become.

The day passed slowly. I think we both dozed off once or twice.

Around lunchtime, we ran to the stream in the

woods for water. Some fleas still nipped at my skin. And I thought a cool dip in the stream might help.

We returned to our spot under the shady birch. Now we were both starving.

"Maybe we can find some scraps of food at my house — in the garbage," I suggested.

"Yuck! I'm not eating garbage," Fergie wailed. "No way." But she knew we had no choice.

We returned to my house and quietly made our way to the side door, where Dad stored the garbage pails.

As we sniffed around for some food, Mickey and my parents opened the back door and stepped out into the yard.

"I'm telling you, Mom!" Mickey cried. "They're ghost dogs! They walked right through my bedroom wall! They're not normal!"

"Save your jokes for Cooper," my father snapped.

"Hey, Fergie, maybe Mickey can help us," I suggested, watching my brother. "He's the only one who believes we're not normal dogs. Maybe we can find a way to tell him who we are."

Fergie sighed. "For sure," she said sarcastically. "Then what? Can you see your parents' faces when Mickey tells them the two dogs hanging around their house are really Cooper and Margaret Ferguson?"

I hung my head. Fergie was right. They'd never believe Mickey, either.

"Well, we have to do *something*!" I said, scratching behind my ear. "These fleas are driving me crazy! I can't live like this!"

"Maybe we can get you a flea collar," Fergie suggested.

"Oh, right. I'll just trot into the Main Street drugstore, put five dollars on the counter, and ask for a flea collar. Nobody will think that's weird." I rolled my eyes.

Fergie snapped at me. "Well, excuse me, Cooper. I was only trying to help!"

Fergie and I spent the rest of the day snapping at each other, getting on each other's nerves.

When dinnertime rolled around, my stomach rumbled loudly. Then I smelled the most wonderful smell.

I raised my nose high in the air and sniffed excitedly.

I'd know that aroma anywhere.

Liver! The leftover liver from last night!

"Come on!" I barked to Fergie. "I've got to get some of that liver!"

We trotted over to the back door and peered inside. My whole family had gathered around the table, ready to eat.

"You're drooling," Fergie said to me in disgust. "Gross."

Like I cared.

I couldn't take my eyes off the plate of liver Mom carried to the table. I watched hungrily as she placed a big slab on my father's plate.

Then she served some to Mickey. Mickey seemed edgy, nervous. I hoped he was still upset from my little trick this morning.

Then Mom placed a piece of liver on the phony Cooper's plate. He jumped from his seat. "Yuck!" he cried out in disgust. "I *hate* liver!"

Mom's jaw dropped. "Cooper! What are you saying? You love liver!"

The phony Cooper began to stutter.

"Oh, uh, did I say I hated it? Oh, no. I'm, uh, just joking, Mom. I love liver. Everyone knows that!"

Mom stared at him suspiciously. "Really, Cooper. You haven't been yourself all day!"

My eyes widened.

This was my chance!

Now was the perfect time to show Mom he *wasn't* himself! He was a total phony!

"I'm going in!" I told Fergie.

I burst through the kitchen door and headed straight for the plate of liver. I'll show Mom who the real Cooper is, I thought happily. The Cooper who loves liver. She'll know it's me instantly!

This has *got* to work.

It's our last chance, I knew. Our only chance.

# 30

Panting excitedly, I charged into the kitchen and leaped up at the table.

Mom screamed and dropped the plate of liver on the floor.

In a flash, I bent down and began lapping it up. Delicious!

"See, Mom? Look, it's me! Your son, Cooper!" I yelped in between bites.

"Sam! Do something! That animal is eating our dinner!"

Huh? Animal? "No, Mom! It's me! Your son! Look, I love liver!"

But it was no use.

All Mom heard was, *"Woof, woof! Woof, woof! Woof, woof! Woof, woof, woof, woof!"*

Dad shoved his chair away from the table and grabbed a newspaper from the counter. He rolled it up, then swatted my nose.

"Ow!"

That hurt!

"I'll see if the line to the pound is still busy," Mom said, picking up the phone. "Try to chase the dogs into the pantry and lock the door. We'll hold them in there until the pound can come get them."

The fake Cooper and Margaret helped Dad back us toward the pantry. "Bad dogs! Bad!" the phony Margaret shouted.

"Dad, do you think the pound will use a tranquilizer gun on them?" the phony Cooper asked.

"Maybe," Dad replied.

I glanced over at Fergie.

Tranquilizer guns? No thank you!

I never ran so fast in all my life. I even ran faster than Fergie.

"Got any other bright ideas, fleabag?" she asked when we were safely in the woods.

I growled at her and turned away. The sun was setting over the trees. The air felt cool. It would be dark soon.

"And thanks for saving some of that liver for me," Fergie snapped. "I'm hungry, too, you know!"

I ignored her.

I gazed longingly through the trees. Through

the window of my house as Mom and Dad washed the dishes.

I couldn't help myself. I felt so bad. I started whimpering.

If only I could be inside my warm, comfortable house right now. In a short while, it would be dark. I didn't want to spend a night in the woods.

Think, Cooper! Think! I urged myself. There must be a way to get our human bodies back.

"Whoa! Wait a minute!" I cried. "I just thought of something!"

Fergie awoke from a nap. "What?" she asked lazily.

"We're dogs, right?"

"Right."

"So we should act like dogs!"

Fergie narrowed her eyes. "Cooper, what are you talking about?"

I took a deep breath. "Okay, listen," I explained. "Remember how those ghost dogs got us out to the shack?"

Fergie nodded.

"That's what we should do! We should pull those kids back there, the way they pulled us! That's what dogs would do!"

Fergie raised her head. Her ears perked up. "Not bad! Not bad at all!"

"We're dogs," I continued. "We have sharp teeth, right? Very sharp teeth. We'll drag them into the woods and into the Changing Room — and before you know it, we'll be Cooper and Fergie again!"

Fergie bounced up and began panting happily and wagging her tail. "Excellent!" she cried.

"Okay, here's the plan." With my paw, I drew a diagram in the dirt. "The phonies are here, in the den. We'll walk through the wall and haul them out through the kitchen door. It's okay if Mom and Dad follow. We can outrun them."

"I'm ready. Let's do it!" Fergie exclaimed.

We trotted to the house and pushed through the wall, as planned.

Inside, the fake Cooper and Fergie were watching MTV on the den TV. We burst through the den wall and surprised them.

"Mom!" the fake Cooper screamed at the top of his lungs. "Dad! Help! It's the dogs!"

Fergie and I moved in on them, snarling as ferociously as we knew how.

I clamped on to the fake Cooper's ankle just as my parents and Mickey burst into the room. I motioned to Fergie to get on with it. In a flash, she leaped on to the phony Fergie and clamped her jaws around her wrist.

Then we tugged.

"Mom! Dad! Help!" the phony Cooper yelled.

"Mr. Holmes!" the phony Fergie cried. "Do something! They're attacking us!"

Mom ran for the broom. But before Dad could swing into action, Fergie and I had dragged the imposters through the kitchen.

I caught a glimpse of Mickey as I tugged. He was hiding in the corner, shaking all over.

Too bad I didn't have time to enjoy that picture.

We were out the door now. Everything was working perfectly. Fergie and I would be back to normal in no time.

The phonies knew where we were taking them. But there was nothing they could do about it. Fergie and I were too strong, too ferocious.

"Dad! Help!" the fake Cooper cried again.

"Don't worry!" Dad called out to him. "The dogs don't seem to want to hurt you! I think they want us to follow them!"

Way to go, Dad!

A short while later, I spotted the clearing where the old shack stood. It won't be long now, I thought happily. In a few minutes, Fergie and I will walk home with my parents. On two legs. No more fleas. No more food from garbage pails. I couldn't wait!

We panted wildly as the struggling imposters attempted to break free. But Fergie and I held on to them for dear life, tugging them, tugging with all our canine strength.

And, then, finally, we were there. The old shack. We pushed the phonies up against the door.

I released the fake Cooper from my grip for a second. I had no choice. I had to scratch a flea.

The phony tried to make a run for it.

"Cooper! He's getting away!" Fergie barked.

"No way!" I barked back. I bounded off after him and clamped my jaws down on the hem of his shirt. Then I dragged him back to the shack.

The fake Fergie screamed with all her might. "No! No! Not in there again!"

I glared up at her.

"Hold on, Margaret," I heard Mom call. "Don't be afraid. Let's see what the dogs are trying to show us."

It was time. Time to make the switch.

"Now!" I yelped.

Fergie and I jumped on the imposters and sent them tumbling into the shack. Then we leaped in after them.

All four of us fell down, down, down. Down into the solid blackness.

Once again, I felt dizzy and warm.

Warmer. Warmer. As if the warm blanket were being pulled over me.

I could feel myself changing. Changing in the darkness, in the sweltering heat.

I gazed above my head. A glowing shadow hovered over me. A shadow with tiny red eyes.

My body shuddered. I began to shake.

And all at once I knew. Something wasn't right.

"Fergie!" I cried out in a harsh whisper. "It's not working! Something is wrong! Something is very wrong!"

# 31

"Cooper!" my mom cried happily, running toward the shack with outstretched arms. "Are you okay?"

"Margaret, what happened in there?" Dad called. "What happened to the dogs?"

"We're okay," Margaret muttered. "It's just an empty shack. That's all."

"I'm going to call the pound again as soon as we get home," Mom announced. "Those dogs shouldn't be allowed to roam free. They're dangerous!"

"Let's just get out of here, okay, Dad?" Cooper said.

Fergie nodded in agreement. "We're okay, Let's go home."

"What an adventure!" Mom sighed.

"At least it isn't boring up here in our new home," Dad added.

"For sure," Cooper agreed.

"What happened?" I asked, rubbing my eyes.

I watched my parents walking away from the shack, their arms around two kids.

"Hey! Those kids!" I cried. "They're not us!"

The door to the shack opened, and two black Labs stumbled out in a daze. Their eyes met, then they bolted away, barking frantically.

What's their problem? I wondered.

I watched the dogs disappear into the trees.

What's going on? I asked myself, totally confused.

I'm not a kid — and I'm not a dog, either!

"Hey, Fergie? Fergie?"

Where *was* she?

When she popped up next to me, we both gasped.

"Oh, no! Please — no! No! No! Noooo!" she wailed.

Her head cocked to one side, and her little brown nose twitched furiously.

"Tell me we're *not*!" I begged her. "Please, Fergie — tell me we're not . . ."

"We *are*!" Fergie squeaked. "We . . . we're *chipmunks*!"

We both squeaked and chittered our surprise.

Fergie gazed down at her furry little body. "How did this happen, Cooper? How did this happen?"

"The woods are filled with chipmunks," I sighed. "Two of them must have wandered into the Changing Room. And we — "

"We switched with the chipmunks — not the kids!" Fergie cried. Her bushy tail thumped furiously on the ground.

I examined my tiny black paws. I moved my teeny little fingers. I twitched my button nose.

Cute. I was so cute!

"Now what?" Fergie wailed. "What do we do now?"

"Uh . . . hunt for acorns?" I suggested.

Fergie's beady little eyes squinted into mine. "Excuse me?"

"Let's hunt for acorns!" I said. "I'm starving!"

Add *more*

# Goosebumps®

to your collection . . .

Here's a chilling preview of

## THE HORROR AT CAMP JELLYJAM

# 3

Elliot's face filled with confusion. He didn't understand me. Or maybe he didn't believe me!

"The trailer has come loose!" I screamed, staring out the bouncing window. "We're rolling downhill — on our own!"

"N-n-n-no!" Elliot chattered. He wasn't stuttering. He was bouncing so hard, he could barely speak. His sneakers hopped so hard on the trailer floor, he seemed to be tap dancing.

"OW!" I let out a pained shriek as my head bounced against the ceiling. Elliot and I stumbled to the back. Gripping the windowsill tightly, I struggled to see where we were heading.

The road curved steeply downhill, through thick pine woods on both sides. The trees were a bouncing blur of greens and browns as we hurtled past.

Picking up speed. Bouncing and tumbling.

Faster.

Faster.

The tires roared beneath us. The trailer tilted and dipped.

I fell to the floor. Landed hard on my knees. Reached to pull myself up. But the trailer swayed, and I went sprawling on my back.

Pulling myself to my knees, I saw Elliot bouncing around on the floor like a soccer ball. I threw myself at the back of the trailer and peered out the window.

The trailer bumped hard. The road curved sharply — but we didn't curve with it!

We shot off the side of the road. Swerved into the trees.

"Elliot!" I shrieked. "We're going to crash!"

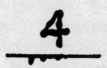

# 4

The trailer jolted hard. I heard a cracking sound.

It's going to break in half! I thought.

I pressed both hands against the front and stared out the window. Dark trees flew past.

A hard bump sent me sprawling to the floor.

I heard Elliot calling my name. "Wendy! Wendy! Wendy!"

I shut my eyes and tensed every muscle. And waited for the crash.

Waited . . .

Waited . . .

Silence.

I opened my eyes. It took me a few seconds to realize that we were no longer moving. I took a deep breath and climbed to my feet.

"Wendy?" I heard Elliot's weak cry from the back of the trailer.

My legs were trembling as I turned around. My

whole body felt weird. As if we were still bouncing. "Elliot — are you okay?"

He had been thrown into one of the bottom bunks. "Yeah. I guess," he replied. He lowered his feet to the floor and shook his head. "I'm kind of dizzy."

"Me, too," I confessed. "What a ride!"

"Better than Space Mountain!" Elliot exclaimed. He climbed to his feet. "Let's get *out* of this thing!"

We both started to the door at the front. It was an uphill climb. The trailer tilted up.

I reached the door first. I grabbed the handle.

A loud knock on the door made me jump back. "Hey . . . !" I cried.

Three more knocks.

"It's Mom and Dad!" Elliot cried. "They found us! Open it up! Hurry!"

He didn't have to tell me to hurry. My heart skipped. I was so glad to see them!

I turned the handle, pushed open the trailer door —

— and gasped.

# 5

I stared into the face of a blond-haired man. His blue eyes sparkled in the bright sunlight.

He was dressed all in white. He wore a crisp white T-shirt tucked into baggy white shorts. A small round button pinned to his T-shirt read **ONLY THE BEST** in bold black letters.

"Uh . . . hi," I finally managed to choke out.

He flashed me a gleaming smile. He seemed to have about two thousand teeth. "Hey, guys — everyone okay in there?" he asked. His blue eyes sparkled even brighter.

"Yeah. We're okay," I told him. "A little shaken up, but — "

"Who are *you?*" Elliot cried, poking his head out the door.

The guy's smile didn't fade. "My name is Buddy."

"I'm Wendy. He's Elliot. We thought you were

our parents," I explained. I hopped down to the ground.

Elliot followed me. "Where are Mom and Dad?" he asked, frowning.

"I haven't seen anyone, guy," Buddy told him. He studied the trailer. "What happened here? You came unhitched?"

I nodded, brushing my dark hair off my face. "Yeah. On the steep hills, I guess."

"Dangerous," Buddy muttered. "You must have been really scared."

"Not me!" Elliot declared.

What a kid. First, he's shaking in terror and calling out my name over and over. Now he's Mister Macho.

"I've never been so scared in all my life!" I admitted.

I took a few steps away from the trailer and searched the woods. The trees creaked and swayed in a light breeze. The sun beamed down brightly. I shielded my eyes with one hand as I peered around.

No sign of Mom and Dad. I couldn't see the highway through the thick trees.

I could see the tire tracks our trailer had made through the soft dirt. Somehow we had shot through a clear path between the trees. The trailer had come to rest at the foot of a sharp, sloping hill.

"Wow. We were lucky," I muttered.

"You're very lucky," Buddy declared cheerfully. He stepped up beside me, placed his hands on my shoulders, and turned me around. "Check it out. Look where you guys landed!"

Gazing up the hill, I saw a wide clearing between the trees. And then I saw a huge, red-and-white banner, stretched high on two poles. I had to squint to read the words on the banner.

Elliot read them aloud: "King Jellyjam's Sports Camp."

"The camp is on the other side of the hill," Buddy told us, flashing us both a friendly smile. "Come on! Follow me!"

"But — but — " my brother sputtered. "We have to find our parents!"

"Hey — no problem, guy. You can wait for them at the camp," Buddy assured him.

"But how will they know where to find us?" I protested. "Should we leave a note?"

Buddy flashed me another dazzling smile. "No. I'll take care of it," he told me. "No problem."

He stepped past the trailer and started up the hill. His white T-shirt and white shorts gleamed in the sunlight. I saw that his socks and high-tops were sparkling white, too.

That's his uniform. He must work at the camp, I decided.

Buddy turned back. "You guys coming?" He

motioned with both hands. "Come on. You're going to like it!"

Elliot and I hurried to catch up to him. My legs trembled as I ran. I could still feel the trailer floor bouncing and jolting beneath me. I wondered if I would ever feel normal again.

As we made our way up the grassy hill, the red-and-white banner came into clearer view. "King Jellyjam's Sports Camp," I read the words aloud.

A funny, purple cartoon character had been drawn beside the words on the banner. He looked like a blob of grape bubble gum. He had a big smile on his face. He wore a gold crown on his head.

"Who's *that*?" I asked Buddy.

Buddy glanced up at the banner. "That's King Jellyjam," he replied. "He's our little mascot."

"Weird-looking mascot for a *sports* camp," I declared, staring up at the purple, blobby king.

Buddy didn't reply.

"Do you work at the camp?" Elliot asked.

Buddy nodded. "It's a great place to work. I'm the head counselor, guys. So — welcome!"

"But we can't go to your camp," I protested. "We have to find our parents. We have to . . ."

Buddy put a hand on my shoulder and a hand on Elliot's shoulder. He guided us up the hill. "You guys have had a close call. You might as well stay and have some fun. Enjoy the camp. Until I can hook up with your parents."

As we neared the top of the hill, I heard voices. Kids' voices. Shouting and laughing.

The clearing narrowed. Tall pine trees, birch trees, and maples clustered over the hill.

"What kind of sports camp is it?" Elliot asked Buddy.

"We play all kinds of sports," Buddy replied. "From Ping-Pong to football. From croquet to soccer. We have swimming. We have tennis. We have archery. We even have a marbles tournament!"

"Sounds like a cool place!" my brother declared, grinning at me.

"Only the best!" Buddy said, slapping Elliot on the shoulder.

I reached the top of the hill first and peered down through the trees to the camp. It seemed to stretch for miles!

I could see two long, white, two-story buildings on either side. Between them, I saw several playing fields, a baseball diamond, a long row of tennis courts, and two enormous swimming pools.

"Those long, white buildings are the dorms," Buddy explained, pointing. "That's the girls' dorm, and that's the boys'. You guys can stay in them while you're here."

"Wow! It looks awesome!" Elliot exclaimed. "Two swimming pools!"

"Olympic size," Buddy told him. "We have diving competitions, too. Are you into diving?"

"Only inside the trailer!" I joked.

"Wendy is into swimming," Elliot told Buddy.

"I think there's a four-lap swim race this afternoon," Buddy told me. "I'll check the schedule for you."

The sun beamed on us as we followed the path down the hill. The back of my neck started to prickle. A cool swim sounded pretty good to me.

"Can anyone sign up for baseball?" Elliot asked Buddy. "I mean, do you have to be on a team or something?"

"You can play any sport you want," Buddy told him. "The only rule at King Jellyjam's Sports Camp is to try hard." Buddy tapped the button on his T-shirt. "Only The Best," he said.

The breeze blew my hair back over my face. "I *knew* I should have had it cut before vacation! I decided I'd have to find something to tie it back with as soon as I got into the dorm.

A soccer match was underway on the nearest field. Whistles blew. Kids shouted. I saw a long row of archery targets at the far end of the soccer field.

Buddy started jogging toward the field. Elliot stepped up beside me. "Hey — we wanted to go to camp, right?" he said, grinning. "Well? We made it!"

Before I could reply, he trotted after Buddy.

I brushed back my hair one more time, then followed. But I stopped when I saw a little girl poke her head out from behind a wide tree trunk.

She appeared to be about six or seven. She had bright red hair and a face full of freckles. She wore a pale blue T-shirt pulled down over black tights.

"Hey — " she called in a loud whisper. "Hey — !"

I turned toward her, startled.

"Don't come in!" she called. "Run away! Don't come in!"

# About the Author

R.L. STINE is the author of the series *Fear Street*, *Nightmare Room*, *Give Yourself Goosebumps*, and the phenomenally successful *Goosebumps*. His thrilling teen titles have sold more than 250 million copies internationally — enough to earn him a spot in the *Guinness Book of World Records*! Mr. Stine lives in New York City with his wife, Jane, and his son, Matt.

# Thrills and chills to make your skin crawl... Don't you want to collect them all?

# Goosebumps®

- ☐ The Abominable Snowman of Pasadena
- ☐ The Barking Ghost
- ☐ The Cuckoo Clock of Doom
- ☐ The Curse of the Mummy's Tomb
- ☐ Deep Trouble
- ☐ Egg Monsters from Mars
- ☐ Ghost Beach
- ☐ Ghost Camp
- ☐ The Ghost Next Door
- ☐ The Haunted Mask
- ☐ The Horror at Camp Jellyjam
- ☐ How I Got My Shrunken Head
- ☐ How to Kill a Monster

- ☐ It Came from Beneath the Sink!
- ☐ Let's Get Invisible!
- ☐ Monster Blood
- ☐ Night of the Living Dummy
- ☐ One Day at HorrorLand
- ☐ Say Cheese and Die!
- ☐ The Scarecrow Walks at Midnight
- ☐ A Shocker on Shock Street
- ☐ Stay Out of the Basement
- ☐ Welcome to Camp Nightmare
- ☐ Welcome to Dead House
- ☐ The Werewolf of Fever Swamp

# Available Wherever Books Are Sold

# Goosebumps®

## Would You Dare Visit a Place That Ghosts, Mummies, Vampires, and Other Creepy Creatures Call Home?

# www.scholastic.com/ goosebumps/books

THE MONSTER MOB

ACTIVITIES

AUTHOR INFO

AND MORE!

## Once you're there, you may never come back.

GBWT

# Fun and Fright, Day or Night

# Goosebumps®

**Each Book $4.99**

____ 0-439-56824-2  Goosebumps: The Abominable Snowman of Pasadena

____ 0-439-56825-0  Goosebumps: The Barking Ghost

____ 0-439-56826-9  Goosebumps: The Cuckoo Clock of Doom

____ 0-439-56827-7  Goosebumps: The Curse of the Mummy's Tomb

____ 0-439-56828-5  Goosebumps: Deep Trouble

____ 0-439-56829-3  Goosebumps: Egg Monsters from Mars

____ 0-439-56830-7  Goosebumps: Ghost Beach

____ 0-439-56831-5  Goosebumps: Ghost Camp

____ 0-439-56832-3  Goosebumps: The Ghost Next Door

____ 0-439-56833-1  Goosebumps: The Haunted Mask

____ 0-439-56834-X  Goosebumps: The Horror at Camp Jellyjam

____ 0-439-56835-8  Goosebumps: How I Got My Shrunken Head

____ 0-439-56836-6  Goosebumps: How to Kill a Monster

____ 0-439-56837-4  Goosebumps: It Came from Beneath the Sink!

____ 0-439-56838-2  Goosebumps: Let's Get Invisible!

____ 0-439-56839-0  Goosebumps: Monster Blood

____ 0-439-56840-4  Goosebumps: Night of the Living Dummy

____ 0-439-56841-2  Goosebumps: One Day at HorrorLand

____ 0-439-56842-0  Goosebumps: Say Cheese and Die!

____ 0-439-56843-9  Goosebumps: The Scarecrow Walks at Midnight

____ 0-439-56844-7  Goosebumps: A Shocker on Shock Street

____ 0-439-56845-5  Goosebumps: Stay Out of the Basement

____ 0-439-56846-3  Goosebumps: Welcome to Camp Nightmare

____ 0-439-56847-1  Goosebumps: Welcome to Dead House

____ 0-439-56848-X  Goosebumps: The Werewolf of Fever Swamp

## Available Wherever Books Are Sold, or Use This Order Form

### Scholastic Inc., P.O. Box 7502, Jefferson City, MO 65102

Please send me the books I have checked above. I am enclosing $_____ (please add $2.00 to cover shipping and handling). Send check or money order—no cash or C.O.D.s please.

Name_____Birth date_____

Address_____

City_____State/Zip_____

Please allow four to six weeks for delivery. Offer good in U.S.A. only. Sorry, mail orders are not available to residents of Canada. Prices subject to change.

▲ SCHOLASTIC

GBOC

# Other Series Worth Screaming About...

## Garth Nix
### The Keys to the Kingdom

The key to a house no one can see—and a mystery that must be solved.

## Emily Rodda
### DELTORA QUEST

A land of magic—and monsters.

## Emily Rodda
### DELTORA SHADOWLANDS

An epic fight against forces of darkness.

## K.A. Applegate
### REMNANTS[T]

The end of the world has come...and gone.

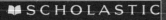

**SCHOLASTIC**

FANT